AUGUST STRINDBERG (1849-1912) is best known outside Sweden as a dramatist, the author of the great Naturalistic dramas *Miss Julie* and *The Father*, and of the pioneering Expressionist dramas *To Damascus* and *A Dreamplay*. But he was also a prolific writer of novels, short stories, essays, journalism and poetry, as well as being a notable artist and photographer. Although he spent many years abroad, Strindberg was born, grew up and died in Stockholm, and many of his summers were spent out among the thousands of islands in the Stockholm Archipelago. The islands, particularly Kymmendö, provided him with the background for a number of his stories and novels and it is Kymmendö that provides the setting and inspiration for *The People of Hemsö*, this roistering tragicomedy of life among the fishermen/ farmers of the archipelago. The novel has rightly become one of Strindberg's most popular works and a great classic of Swedish literature.

PETER GRAVES has translated works by Linnaeus, Jacob Wallenberg, August Strindberg, Selma Lagerlöf and Peter Englund, and he has been awarded a number of translation prizes. Before retiring he was Head of the School of Literatures, Languages and Cultures at the University of Edinburgh, where he taught Swedish.

Some other books from Norvik Press

Juhani Aho: *The Railroad* (translated by Owen Witesman)

Kjell Askildsen: *A Sudden Liberating Thought* (translated by Sverre Lyngstad)

Victoria Benedictsson: *Money* (translated by Sarah Death)

Hjalmar Bergman: *Memoirs of a Dead Man* (translated by Neil Smith)

Jens Bjørneboe: *Moment of Freedom* (translated by Esther Greenleaf Mürer)

Jens Bjørneboe: *Powderhouse* (translated by Esther Greenleaf Mürer)

Jens Bjørneboe: *The Silence* (translated by Esther Greenleaf Mürer)

Johan Borgen: *The Scapegoat* (translated by Elizabeth Rokkan)

Kerstin Ekman: *Witches' Rings* (translated by Linda Schenck)

Kerstin Ekman: *The Spring* (translated by Linda Schenck)

Kerstin Ekman: *The Angel House* (translated by Sarah Death)

Kerstin Ekman: *City of Light* (translated by Linda Schenck)

Arne Garborg: *Tha Making of Daniel Braut* (translated by Marie Wells)

Svava Jakobsdóttir, *Gunnlöth's Tale* (translated by Oliver Watts)

P. C. Jersild: *A Living Soul* (translated by Rika Lesser)

Selma Lagerlöf: *Lord Arne's Silver* (translated by Sarah Death)

Selma Lagerlöf: *The Löwensköld Ring* (translated by Linda Schenck)

Selma Lagerlöf: *The Phantom Carriage* (translated by Peter Graves)

Viivi Luik: *The Beauty of History* (translated by Hildi Hawkins)

Henry Parland: *To Pieces* (translated by Dinah Cannell)

Amalie Skram: *Lucie* (translated by Katherine Hanson and Judith Messick)

Amalie and Erik Skram: *Caught in the Enchanter's Net: Selected Letters* (edited and translated by Janet Garton)

August Strindberg: *Tschandala* (translated by Peter Graves)

August Strindberg: *The Red Room* (translated by Peter Graves)

Hjalmar Söderberg: *Martin Birck's Youth* (translated by Tom Ellett)

Hjalmar Söderberg: *Selected Stories* (translated by Carl Lofmark)

Anton Tammsaare: *The Misadventures of the New Satan* (translated by Olga Shartze and Christopher Moseley)

Elin Wägner: *Penwoman* (translated by Sarah Death)

THE PEOPLE OF HEMSÖ

A Story from the Islands

by

August Strindberg

Translated from the Swedish
and with an afterword by
Peter Graves

Norvik Press
2012

Originally published in Swedish by Albert Bonniers Förlag under the title of *Hemsöborna* (1887).

This translation and introduction © Peter Graves 2012
The translator's moral right to be identified as the translator of the work has been asserted.

Norvik Press Series B: English Translations of Scandinavian Literature, no. 54

ISBN: 978-1-870041-95-9

Norvik Press gratefully acknowledges the generous support of Kulturrådet (Swedish Arts Council) towards the publication of this translation.

Norvik Press
Department of Scandinavian Studies
University College London
Gower Street
London WC1E 6BT
United Kingdom
Website: www.norvikpress.com
E-mail address: norvik.press@ucl.ac.uk

Managing editors: Sarah Death, Helena Forsås-Scott, Janet Garton, C. Claire Thomson.

Cover illustration: *På havet* (1889) by Albert Gustav Aristides Edelfelt (Göteborgs konstmuseum).

Layout: Elettra Carbone
Cover design: Elettra Carbone
Printed in the UK by Lightning Source UK Ltd.

Contents

CHAPTER I

Carlsson takes a job and is found to be a bit of a chancer

He came like a snowstorm one April evening and had an earthenware jug hanging on a strap round his neck. Clara and Lotten had gone in the herring boat to pick him up but it was ages before they got back to the boat. They had to go to the store for a barrel of tar and to the chemist's for grey salve for the pig and to the post to buy a stamp and then down to Fia Lövström's at Kroken to borrow a cockerel in return for a couple of pounds of twine for making nets and finally they had ended up in the inn, where Carlsson treated them to coffee and cakes. At last they were back at the boat and now Carlsson wanted to take the helm, which he could not, never having seen a square-rigger before, but he yelled at them anyway to hoist the foresail – which the boat did not have.

Pilots and porters stood there on the customs quay grinning at all their manoeuvrings as the boat went about and ran before the wind down towards Saltsäcken.

'Hey, you there, there's a hole in your boat!' an apprentice pilot yelled into the wind. 'Put a bung in it!' When Carlsson looked for the hole, Clara shoved him aside and took over the rudder while Lotten took the oars and managed to turn the boat into the wind again, and then they bore off down towards Aspösund at a good pace.

Carlsson was a small, solidly-built Värmlander with blue eyes and a nose as crooked as a clasp-hook. He was lively, full of fun and inquisitive, but he had no idea about anything to do with the sea. He was being brought to Hemsö to tend the fields and the animals, which no one else had wanted anything to do with ever since old Flod had passed away, leaving his widow in sole charge of the farm.

Now Carlsson started trying to pump the girls for information about life on the island but he got nothing but typical islanders' answers:

'Well now, I don't know about that! Well now, I couldn't say! Well now, I really don't know!'

So there was nothing to be got out of them.

Long-tailed duck quacked behind the rocks and blackcock crooned in the sprucewoods as the boat splashed along between rocky islets and skerries, crossing bays and narrows until darkness fell and the stars came out one by one. Then it was out into open water, where the Huvudskär lighthouse was flashing. Here and there they slipped past a broom-beacon, sometimes a ghostly white sailing-mark, in some places late snowdrifts shone like linen on a bleaching green, in others net-floats rose to the surface of the black water and scraped against the keel as the boat passed over them. A dozing gull rose startled from its rocky perch, its cries wakening terns and gulls that set up a hellish din, while far, far out, where the stars met the sea, they could see the red and green eyes of a great steamer with a long row of round lights shining out through the portholes of the saloon.

Everything was new to Carlsson and he asked about everything. And now the answers started coming, so many of them that it became apparent to him that he was in alien territory. He was a landlubber, and so the islanders viewed him in the same way as townspeople view country yokels.

The water slapped at the yoal as it moved into sheltered water and they had to lower the sail and row, which quickly brought them into another sound from where they could see a light shining from a cottage in among alder trees and pines.

'Here we are – home,' Clara said as the boat shot through a channel cleared through the reeds into a narrow bay, with the reeds rustling against the gunwales and disturbing a spawning pike that was being tempted by a baited hook.

The farm mongrel started barking and a lantern could be

seen moving around up by the cottage.

In the meantime they moored the boat to the end of the jetty and began to unload. The sail was rolled on the yard-arm, the mast taken down and the stays and shroud pins wound around it. The tar barrel was trundled ashore and soon the jetty was covered with bundles, jugs, baskets and packages.

Carlsson looked about him in the half-light and everything he saw was new and unfamiliar. There was a fish-cage dangling on a winch from the jetty, along the length of which ran a railing for hanging floats, painters, grappling irons, weights, lines, long-lines and hooks, while herring casks, troughs, creels, vats, tubs and line-boxes were stacked on the planking. In the boathouse at the end of the jetty, stuffed eider, goosander, red merganser, velvet scoter and goldeneye hung ready to be used as wildfowling decoys, and on brackets under the eaves rested sails and masts, oars, boathooks, rowlocks, balers, ice-picks and burbot clubs. The drying-frames on the shore were draped with herring-nets as big as the grandest church windows, flounder nets with mesh large enough to put an arm through, and perch nets as new and white as the finest sleigh net. Two rows of forked poles, running straight up from the jetty like the avenue to a manor house, were used to hang the great trawl-net, and at the far end of this avenue a lantern was moving. Its light shone down on the sandy path, making the mussel shells and dried fish gills sparkle and the herring scales stuck to the nets glisten like hoar-frost on a spider's web. But the lantern also lit up the face of an old woman, her complexion dried by the wind but with two small, kind eyes that years of staring into an open fire had made narrow. The dog ran ahead of her, a shaggy beast as much at home in the sea as on land.

'Bless my soul, you're home at last,' the woman greeted them. 'You've brought the fellow with you, have you?'

'Yes'm, here we are,' Clara answered. 'This is Carlsson.'

The old woman dried her right hand on her apron and held it out to her new farm-hand.

'Welcome, Carlsson, I hope you find it to your liking here. Did you bring the coffee and sugar, girls? The sails have been put away in the shed, have they? Come along, then, and we'll get some food into you.'

The little group walked up the slope, Carlsson silent and curious, waiting to see how life would turn out in this new place.

There was a fire burning in the parlour and the tablecloth on the white, gate-legged table was clean. On the cloth stood an hourglass-shaped schnapps bottle, surrounded by Gustavsberg china cups decorated with roses and forget-me-nots. A newly baked loaf, fresh rusks, a butter dish, sugar bowl and jug of cream completed the table setting, suggesting more prosperity than Carlsson had expected to find out here in the back of beyond. And, on inspection, the room itself looked quite promising. The flickering light from the fire and from a candle in a brass candlestick shone on the slightly scuffed polish of a mahogany bureau, reflected off the varnished case and brass pendulum of a wall-clock, sparkled on the silver inlay of the long, damascened barrels of several fowling pieces and picked out the gilt lettering on the spines of hymn-books and homily-books, almanacs and farming manuals.

'Come along, Carlsson,' the woman said and Carlsson, being a child of the modern age, did not run off and hide in the barn but stepped forward at once and took a seat on the bench while the girls carried his chest through to the kitchen on the other side of the hallway.

Widow Flod took the coffee pot off its hook over the fire, dropped in a piece of dried fish skin to clear the coffee and hung it back to heat up. Then she repeated her invitation, this time adding that Carlsson should sit at the table.

Carlsson sat there twisting his cap in his hands and watching to see which way the wind was blowing before setting his sails. It was obvious that he had determined to get on the right side of his mistress, but since he could not yet decide whether she was the sort of woman who would tolerate chit-chat he did not want to risk nattering until he could see how the land lay.

'That's a very nice bureau you've got there,' he tried for a start, fingering the brass roses on it.

'Hm!' said the widow, 'not that there's much in it.'

'Oh, I wouldn't be so sure about that,' Carlsson said in a flattering tone and poked his little finger into the keyhole in the lid. 'Plenty of dinero in there, I bet!'

'We bought it at auction and there was a time when there was a bob or two in it, but what with burying Flod and Gusten serving his time in the army and the farm going from bad to worse... Then they went and built that new house – no use to man nor beast! So it's all trickled out bit by bit. Take some sugar and have a cup of coffee now.'

'Shall I go first?' Carlsson asked in an ingratiating voice.

'Yes, there's no one else at home,' she answered. 'That blessed boy is out wildfowling again and he's taken Norman with him as well, so nothing will get done. Any chance of some fowling and off he goes, leaving the cattle and the fishing to go to rack and ruin. That's why you're here, Carlsson, you see, to get things back on an even keel. You'll need to keep an eye on the boys, be a cut above them, so to speak. Won't you have a rusk, Carlsson?'

'Well, yes'm, but if I'm supposed to be a cut above the rest and they're supposed to obey me, there'll need to be some discipline and I'm going to need some backing. I know what lads are like once you get too matey with them,' Carlsson said, moving in quickly now he was getting the gist of things. 'As to the seafaring side of things, I won't interfere because I know nothing about it, but on land, that's where I know my stuff and that's where I must be in charge.'

'Yes, we can see about all that tomorrow – it's Sunday and we can talk about it by the light of day. Have a dram now, Carlsson, and then you can go to bed.'

She gave him another cup of coffee and Carlsson picked up the hour-glass bottle and poured himself a good quarter of a cupful. After taking a swig he felt disposed to resume the previous conversation, which he had been finding more than a little agreeable. The old woman, however, had got up and was fiddling with the fire, the girls were scuttering in and out, and then the dog started barking in the yard, catching everyone's attention.

'Aha, that must be the boys back,' Madame Flod said.

Voices could be heard outside, accompanied by the clatter of hobnails on the stones. Peering through the Busy Lizzies on the window sill, Carlsson saw the outline of two men in the moonlight, gun barrels poking above their shoulders and packs on their backs.

The dog barked in the hallway and the parlour door opened. In strode the son of the house wearing sea-boots and a reefer jacket and, with the confident pride of the successful hunter, he tossed his game-bag and a brace of eider on the table by the door.

'Evening, mother! Here's some meat for you!' he greeted her without noticing the newcomer.

'Good evening, Gusten, you've been out a long time,' she answered, looking with grudging pleasure at the fine eider drakes with their coal-black and chalk-white plumage, pinkish breasts and sea-green necks. 'I see the shooting was good. Now Gusten, this is Carlsson, the man we've been waiting for!'

With his small sharp eyes half concealed by pale red eyelashes her son gave Carlsson a searching look and his expression changed immediately from open to wary.

'Evening, Carlsson,' he said, short and reserved.

'And good evening to you,' the farm-hand answered, affecting a casual tone but ready to take the upper hand once he had the measure of the young man.

Gusten took a seat at the head of the table with his elbow on the window-sill and let his mother give him a cup of coffee, into which he immediately poured some schnapps. While drinking it he stealthily watched Carlsson, who had picked up the birds and was inspecting them.

'Fine birds, these,' Carlsson said, squeezing the breasts to feel how plump they were. 'I can see you're a good shot – the shots have gone in just right.'

Gusten answered with a sly grin. He could tell straightaway that the farm-hand knew nothing about shooting since he was praising shots that had entered along the lie of the feathers, thus making the birds worthless as decoys.

But Carlsson carried on talking undaunted, praising the sealskin bags, admiring the gun and making a fool of himself by showing his complete ignorance of anything to do with the sea.

'What have you done with Norman?' Madame Flod asked, beginning to get sleepy.

'He's taking the things up to the shed,' Gusten answered, 'but he'll be here soon.'

'Rundqvist's already gone to bed. Well, it's about time, too. You must be tired, Carlsson, after all your travelling, so if you come with me I'll show you where you're to sleep.'

Carlsson would have been happy to stay and help empty the hour-glass bottle but the hints were too obvious to risk succumbing to the temptation. The widow accompanied him out to the kitchen and then quickly returned to her son, whose face had already assumed an open, candid expression again.

'Well, what do you think of him?' she asked. 'He seems a decent, willing sort.'

'Nah!' Gusten pronounced in a long, drawn-out way. 'Don't trust him, mother. He talks a load of rubbish, the bugger!'

'Ah, you're just saying that. He could be a reliable enough fellow even if he is a bit of a chatterbox.'

'Take my word for it, mother, that one's a chancer and we'll have a deal of trouble before we get shot of him. Not that it matters as long as he works for his keep and as long as he stays away from me. I know you never believe anything I say but you'll see, you'll see! And you'll regret it when it's too late. Remember what it was like with old Rundqvist – he could lay on the soft soap but it turned out his back was even softer and now we're stuck with him, probably to his dying day. One thing you can be sure of with smarmy types like this one is that their bellies are as big as their mouths.'

'Gusten, you're just like your father, you know. Always thinking the worst of people, and always asking the impossible. Rundqvist is no seaman, he's a landlubber, but he can do a lot of things the rest of you can't. You know we're never going to get an islander to take the job here because they're all going off to the navy or the customs or the pilot service. It's only mainland people who are prepared to come out here, and we have to take what we can get.'

'Yes, it's obvious no one wants to work on a farm any more, they all want a Crown job – so all the flotsam and jetsam from the mainland washes up out here. No chance of decent people coming out to the skerries unless they've got a good reason to. Which is why I said what I said before: keep your eyes open!'

'Right enough, Gusten, and you should keep your eyes open too and watch out for what's yours,' his mother said. 'It's all going to be yours after all, so you should stay at home more and not be out wildfowling all the time. At the very least, you shouldn't be taking people away from their work the way you do.'

Gusten plucked at one of the eider before answering.

'Oh all right, mother, but you know you like a roast on the table when there's been nothing but salt pork and dried fish all winter, so don't go on about it. It's not as if I waste my time in the alehouse, so I deserve some fun somewhere. We have enough food, don't we, and some money in the bank too, and the house isn't exactly falling down. If it does burn down, so much the better – we've got fire insurance.'

'The house may not be falling apart but everything else is. The fences need mending, the ditches need clearing, the barn roof's rotting away and leaking on the beasts, there's not a jetty that's safe, the boats are as dry as tinder, the nets need tarring and the milk cellar needs a new roof. My, oh my! There's so much needs doing and it never gets done. But now we'll see if we can get it done after all, now we've got someone whose job it is to deal with it. It may well be that Carlsson's just the man for the job.'

'Let him get on with it, then!' Gusten snapped, pushing his fingers through his short-cropped hair so that it stood up in spikes. 'Look, here comes Norman. Come and have a dram, Norman.'

Norman, a short, broad, fair-haired fellow with the

beginnings of a pale moustache and blue eyes, came into the room and sat down by his hunting companion after greeting Madame Flod. As soon as the two heroes had taken their clay pipes from their waistcoat pockets and filled them with Black Anchor, they took a coffee laced with schnapps and began – as hunters do – to go through their exploits out in the skerries shot by shot. They examined the birds, felt the wounds with their fingers, counted the pellets, discussed uncertain shots and made plans for future expeditions.

Carlsson, meanwhile, was out in the kitchen viewing his sleeping quarters.

The kitchen was a log cabin that resembled an upturned boat floating with its keel in the air on top of a cargo of everything under the sun. Nets and fishing equipment hung on beams right up under the sooty roof. Below them boards and planks were stored to dry, together with skeins of flaxen and hemp line, grappling-irons, wrought iron, bunches of onions, tallow candles and wooden provision boxes. A long row of newly stuffed decoys was lined up along one crossbeam, sheepskins were thrown over a second, and from the third dangled sea-boots, knitted jerseys, linen clothing, shirts and stockings. Between the beams ran wooden spits on which rounds of crispbread had been threaded, and there were poles to hold eel-skins and long-lines and ledger tackle.

An unpainted wooden table stood by the gable-end window, and against the walls were three pull-out beds, already made up with fairly clean but coarse sheets.

The widow had pointed Carlsson to a place in one of these and then she had left, taking the candle with her and leaving the newcomer in the weak light provided by the glowing embers in the stove and the small, criss-cross pattern of moonlight on the floor made by the small panes in the window. For the sake of modesty, since the girls also slept in the kitchen, no candles were provided at bedtime and Carlsson began to undress in the gloom. He removed his coat and boots and took his watch from his waistcoat pocket to wind it up by the light of the coals in the stove. He had just put the key in the hole and begun to wind his watch with a rather unpractised hand – he only wound it up on Sundays and special occasions – when he heard a deep, grating voice emerging from the bedclothes.

'Bloody hell, he's even got a watch!'

Carlsson jumped, looked down and in the glow from the fire saw two peering eyes and a tousled head supported on a pair of hairy arms.

'What's it got to do with you?' he responded, never short of an answer.

'The church bell tells you when it's time to go there – not that I ever do,' the head answered. 'You're a posh one, aren't you – morocco leather cuffs on your boots and all!'

'I wouldn't be seen with anything else, *and* I've got galoshes!'

'Jesus, galoshes, too! You can probably run to a dram then?'

'Certainly can, if that's what's needed,' Carlsson answered in a decisive voice and went to fetch his earthenware bottle. 'Here we go, help yourself.'

He pulled out the cork, took a swig and handed over the bottle.

'God bless you, I do believe it's schnapps! Cheers, and welcome to the island! Now we're mates, Carlsson, you can call me Crazy Rundqvist. That's what I'm usually called, anyway.'

And he crept back under the covers.

Carlsson undressed and slipped into bed after hanging his watch on the salt-box and placing his boots in the middle of the floor so the red morocco decoration was visible. The cottage was silent apart from Rundqvist's snuffling over by the stove. Carlsson lay awake thinking of the future. Madame Flod's words that he should consider himself a cut above the others and put the farm back on its feet stuck in his mind like a nail, and his brain ached and throbbed around this nail as if a tumour was forming. He lay and thought of the mahogany bureau and the son's red hair and suspicious eyes. He saw himself walking round with a big bunch of keys on a steel ring and rattling them in his trouser pocket. Then someone comes up to him and asks for money and he lifts his apron, shakes his right leg and feels the keys against his thigh; he picks through the keys like someone picking oakum and when he reaches the smallest key – the one that fits the lid of the bureau – he puts it into the keyhole, just as he had done with his little finger this evening, but the keyhole, that had at first resembled the pupil of an eye, now grows round and big and black like the muzzle of a gun and at the other end of the barrel he can see the son's keen and wily, rudd-red eye taking aim, as if to defend his gold.

Someone came through the kitchen door and Carlsson jerked out of his doze. In the middle of the floor, where the chequerboard of moonlight now lay, stood two white-clad figures who quickly dived into a bed that creaked for some considerable time like a boat against a rickety jetty. Then there was some more wriggling under the sheets, followed by giggling, then silence.

'Goodnight, little girls,' Rundqvist muttered in a sleepy voice. 'Please dream about me.'

'Fat chance of that,' Lotten answered.

'Shush! Don't talk to that horrible old man,' Clara warned.

'You're so sweet, you two. I wish I could be as sweet as you,' Rundqvist sighed. 'Oh God, we just get old and we can't have what we want any more and life's not worth a damn. Goodnight little ones, you'd better keep an eye on Carlsson – he's got a watch *and* morocco boots. What a lucky fellow! Luck can come and luck can pass, it's the lucky man who gets the lass. What are you lying giggling about? Carlsson, Carlsson, can I have another dram? It's hellish cold over here and there's a draught from the stove.'

'No, no more, I'm going to sleep,' snapped Carlsson, whose dreams of the future had been disturbed – a future in which neither wine nor women figured since he had already started being 'a cut above'.

Silence fell again, broken only by the dull murmur of hunters' tales penetrating through two doors and the sound of the night wind gently tugging at the damper in the chimney.

Carlsson closed his eyes and listened half-asleep to Lotten's quiet murmur as she recited by heart something he could not catch at first but which eventually ended in a long, unbroken stream from which he was able to pick out 'andleadusnotinto temptationbutdeliverus   fromevil   forthineisthekingdom thepowerandtheglory   foreverandever   amen.   Goodnight, Clara, sleep well!'

After a short while snores could be heard from the girls' bed and Rundqvist, whether genuinely or as a joke, was driving them home enough to make the windows rattle. Carlsson was lying there dozing, unsure whether he was awake or asleep, when he felt the covers being lifted and a pudgy, sweating body slipped in alongside him.

'It's just me – Norman,' whispered an ingratiating voice and he realised that he was going to have the farm-hand as his bedfellow.

'So the hunter's home from the hill, eh?' croaked Rundqvist in a rusty bass voice. 'And there's me thinking the lad would be out for his Saturday night's hunting.'

'Fine one to talk about hunting, you are, Rundqvist, you haven't got much of a gun left,' Norman hissed.

'Oh, I haven't, have I?' the old man answered, determined to have the last word. 'I can shoot blackbirds with a pop-gun, I can – between the sheets, too.'

'Have you put the fire out in there?' Widow Flod called in a kindly voice through the door from the hallway.

'Yes, yes!' they answered in chorus.

'Goodnight to you, then.'

'Goodnight, mistress.'

There was much sighing and puffing and blowing and snuffling until the snoring started again.

Carlsson, however, lay half-awake for a while longer, counting the window-panes to make his dreams come true.

CHAPTER II

*Sunday rest and Sunday pastimes; the good shepherd and the
naughty sheep; the woodcock that got what was coming to them;
and the farm-hand who got a room.*

When Carlsson woke to the crowing of the cock on Sunday
morning all the beds were empty and the girls were standing
by the stove in their underskirts in the bright sunshine that was
pouring into the kitchen.

Carlsson leapt into his trousers in a flash and went out to
the green to wash. Young Norman was already sitting on a
herring barrel having his hair cut by Rundqvist, a jack-of-all-
trades, who had donned a clean, starched shirt-front the size
of a daily newspaper and was wearing his best boots. They
pointed Carlsson in the direction of an iron cauldron with its
feet missing, which was used as a wash-basin, and there he
performed his Sunday ablutions with a little blob of green
soap.

Gusten's freckled and lathered face was visible in the cottage
window, pulling nasty faces in a piece of mirror known as the
'Sunday peeper', his cut-throat razor glinting in the sunlight as
he ran it back and forth across his face.

'Are you off to church today?' Carlsson asked by way of
morning greeting.

'No, we don't get to the Lord's House that often,' Rundqvist
answered, 'since it's a good few miles to row there and a
good few to row back and we aren't supposed to profane the
Sabbath with unnecessary work, are we?'

Lotten came out to rinse the potatoes and Clara went to the
store-house to fetch salted fish from the winter barrel – known

as the family grave because all the small fish, whatever the species, that died in the net or fish-tank and so would not keep, were salted down in it for the daily needs of the household. Pale roach lay side by side with red rudd, young bream, ruff, lumpfish, perch, small frying pike, flounders, tench, burbot and whitefish, all damaged in some way – torn gills, a hooked-out eye, a badly aimed fish-spear, a boot heel in the middle of the belly and so on. Clara took a couple of handfuls, rinsed away as much salt as possible, and into the pot went the lot of them.

While breakfast was on the fire, Carlsson got dressed and did a round of the hillock to inspect the premises.

The cottage, which was actually two cottages joined together, lay on a rocky knoll at the southern and inner end of a long shallow inlet off the bay. It cut so far inland that the open sea was out of sight and the inlet felt more like a small inland lake. The hillock sloped down to a valley with pastures, meadows and paddocks, all surrounded by a leafy wood of birch, alder and oak. High ground with spruce trees growing on it protected the north side of the bay from the cold winds, and the southern part of the island was cloaked with thickets of pine and birch or mosses and bogs, in among which a field had been ploughed out here and there.

On the knoll beside the cottage was the food-store, and a little way away from it stood the new house, a fairly large, red, cross-timbered, wooden building with a tiled roof. Old Man Flod had built it for his retirement but now it stood unoccupied because his widow had no wish to live there alone. And, in any case, all those unnecessary fireplaces would have taken too great a toll of the woods.

The byre and the barn lay farther away, over towards the paddock. The bath-house and store-cellar lay in the shade of a copse of fine oaks and the roof of a derelict smithy was visible at the far end of the south meadow. The boathouses were down at the landward end of the inlet close to the jetty, and there was also a small harbour for the boats there.

Carlsson was no admirer of the beauty of the district but he seemed pleased with everything he saw. The bay with its good fishing, the level meadows, the sloping, well-drained arable land sheltered from the wind, the dense wood, the fine quality of the timber in the copses – everything promised a good return if only a firm hand could set things in motion and bring all this buried treasure up into the light of day.

After he had sauntered around for a while Carlsson's inspection was interrupted by a ringing 'Halloo!' from the cottage door. It echoed round the bays and inlets and was immediately answered in the same tone from the barn, the paddock and the smithy.

It was Clara calling them to breakfast and the four men were soon sitting round the kitchen table, which was laid with freshly boiled potatoes, salted fish, butter, rye-bread and, it being Sunday, schnapps. Widow Flod was moving round the kitchen, encouraging them all to eat heartily while at the same time keeping an eye on the stove, where a mash was being boiled up for the hens and pigs.

Carlsson took a seat at the top, short end of the table, Gusten had chosen one long side and Rundqvist the other, and Norman was at the other short end, so there was no way of telling who had the seat of honour – they looked like four members of a committee. It was Carlsson, however, who assumed the chairman's role, emphasising his points by banging his fork on the table. He talked about agriculture and cattle, to which Gusten did not respond or, when he did, he responded by talking about fishing and hunting, in which he was supported by Norman. Meanwhile Rundqvist kindled discord even-handedly, adding a faggot of dissension whenever it looked as if there was a glimmer of agreement, fanning the flames when they looked to be dying down, jabbing to the right and to the left and showing the assembled company that he alone knew what he was talking about whereas they were all equally stupid and ignorant.

Gusten avoided answering Carlsson directly, always addressing himself to one of the others instead, and Carlsson soon realised that he was not going to find an ally in Gusten. Norman, the youngest of them, always checked that anything he said had the support of the master of the house – that, after all, was the safest line to take.

'Yes, but fattening pigs when you're getting no milk from the cowshed, there's no value in that,' Carlsson blustered. 'And you won't get milk unless you sow clover with the autumn sowing. And you must rotate the crops you cultivate – rotation, one thing after the other!'

'It's just the same with the fishing, it really is, isn't it, Norman?' Gusten said to his neighbour. 'You can't set the herring nets until the flounders have stopped taking, and you won't get any flounders before the pike have finished spawning. One thing leads to another, doesn't it, and when one thing lets up another starts. That's right, isn't it, Norman?'

Norman agreed willingly and, just to be on the safe side, took up the same refrain when he saw Carlsson getting ready to pitch in again.

'Yes, that's right, one thing starts when another lets up.'

'Who's let off, more like?' Rundqvist thought it appropriate to interpose at this point as Carlsson, with the tail end of a rudd stuck between his teeth, began waving his arms vigorously in an effort to drag the conversation back onto his own ground. He had no choice but to join in with the others' mirth, which arose more from malicious joy in moving the subject away from agriculture than from any appreciation of the simple joke. Encouraged by his success Rundqvist began to embellish on this topic, so all hope of finding an audience for a serious discussion was lost.

Once breakfast was over Madame Flod came in and asked Carlsson and Gusten to accompany her to the byre and the fields to discuss the distribution of tasks and see what was to be done to get the farm back on its feet, after which they were all to meet in the cottage for the Sunday readings.

Rundqvist lay down on the sofa by the stove and lit his pipe while Norman took out his accordion and sat on the porch. The others went up to the byre. Carlsson was more than a little gratified to find that the situation was worse than his worst fears. Twelve cows were down on their knees eating moss and straw because the fodder had run out. All efforts to get them back on their feet were unsuccessful, and after Carlsson and Gusten had tried to lift them with a plank under their bellies they were left to their fate for the time being.

Carlsson shook his head ominously, like a doctor leaving a death-bed, but he chose to keep any good advice and suggestions for improvement to himself until later.

The two oxen were in an even worse state than the cattle since they had just finished the spring ploughing. And the sheep had nothing to nibble but the bark on bundles of twigs from which the leaves had long since been eaten.

The pigs were thin as hunting dogs, hens were running round in the barn, dung-heaps were strewn here and there, and water was left to drain away wherever it could find its own way out.

Once everything had been inspected and found to be in a state of utter dereliction, Carlsson announced that the knife was the only solution.

'Six cows giving milk are better than twelve starving,' he said before examining the udders and flanks and pointing with an air of absolute certainty to the six that should be fattened up and sent for slaughter.

Gusten objected but Carlsson was insistent and asserted that slaughter it must be. 'Slaughter it is, as sure as I live and breathe!'

There had to be other changes, too, but first and foremost they had to buy some good, dry hay for the cattle until they could be let out to graze in the woods.

When Gusten heard that they would have to buy hay he protested vehemently at the thought of spending money on something they could grow themselves, but Madame Flod silenced him by telling him he had no idea what he was talking about.

After making a few minor preliminary arrangements, they left the byre and went out into the fields.

Whole swathes of land were lying fallow.

'Oh Lordy, Lordy, Lordy!' Carlsson mumbled pityingly when

he saw good land being cultivated in such an old-fashioned way. 'Lordy, Lordy, Lordy, how pathetic! No one, no one at all, leaves fields fallow any more, they sow clover. Why grow a crop every second year when you can get one every year?'

Gusten argued that gathering a crop year in and year out exhausted the soil which, after all is said and done, is just like a human being and needs a rest, but Carlsson gave him a correct if somewhat vague explanation of how clover fertilises rather than depletes the soil. As well as keeping it free from weeds.

'Never heard that before, crops that fertilise!' said Gusten, who had failed to understand Carlsson's learned disquisition on how plants of the grass family take most of their nutrition 'from the air'.

Then they inspected the ditches, which were found to be overgrown, badly drained and full of groundwater. The few crops that had been sown were growing in patches here and there, as if the seed had been thrown down in fistfuls, and between these patches weeds flourished undisturbed. The meadows lay there untended, last year's leaves covering the grass and smothering it into a mess of sticky sludge. The fences were ramshackle, bridges were missing and everything was as dilapidated as Madame Flod had described it to Gusten during the previous evening's conversation. But Gusten would not listen to Carlsson's profound observations, sweeping them aside as something unpleasant dug up from the past. He was afraid of all the work they signalled and even more of the amount of money his mother would have to cough up.

By the time they reached the calf paddock Gusten was already lagging behind, and by the time they reached the woods he had disappeared. The widow yelled for him a few times but received no response.

'Oh, let him go,' she said. 'That's Gusten for you – he's always been pretty lackadaisical except when he can go out on the water with his gun. You mustn't think any the worse of him for that, Carlsson, because there's no bad in the boy. It's just that his father wanted better things for him, didn't want him to be a farm-hand, so let him do whatever he enjoyed doing. When he was twelve he got his own boat, and a gun too, of course, and ever since then he's just been out of order. But now that the fishing's not what it was, I have to think more about the farm, which is a safer bet than the sea, when all is said and done. It would all have worked out if only Gusten had known how to manage the farm-workers but, no, he always has to be so pally with the boys and so the work just doesn't get done.'

'Aye, cosying up to the workers gets you nowhere,' Carlsson said, quickly catching her drift. 'I'll tell you this, missus, just between the two of us, if I'm to be any sort of boss, I'm going to have to eat my meals in the parlour and have a room of my own to sleep in. There'll be no respect otherwise, which means I'll get nowhere.'

'Eating in the parlour is out of the question,' the woman said with some alarm as she climbed over the stile. 'Farm-workers nowadays won't put up with anyone eating anywhere but with them in the kitchen. Not even Flod would risk it latterly, and Gusten has never even dared try. If you do try, they'll get on their high horses, make a fuss about the food and start getting thrawn. No, there can be no question of that. But a room to sleep in, that's another matter and we'll see what we can do about that. Everyone thinks there are too many people sleeping in the kitchen as it is, and I imagine Norman would prefer to have the bed to himself rather than having to share it with someone else.'

Carlsson thought it best to content himself with that for the present, half a loaf being better than none.

They had now reached the spruce-wood where a late snow-drift, filthy with dirt and pine-needles, lingered on between a couple of boulders. But the trees were already oozing resin in the blazing April sun and wood-anemones were flowering at their feet. Hepatica were pushing up through the broken mesh of decaying leaves under the hazel-bushes and a warm, damp smell was rising from the hair-cap moss. Through the trees they could see warm air shimmering above the fence round the meadow, and in the distance a gentle breeze darkened the blue of the bay. Squirrels were nibbling away up in the branches and a green woodpecker was hammering and chattering.

Ahead of Carlsson, the widow was skipping along the bare path over pine-needles and roots and, seeing her agile steps and catching glimpses of the soles of her shoes appearing and disappearing under the hem of her dress, he recalled that yesterday he had thought of her as older.

'You're pretty nimble on your feet,' Carlsson said, with an urge to voice his feelings of spring.

'Oh, you're just saying that. Anyone would think you were teasing an old woman.'

'No, I always mean what I say,' Carlsson assured her smoothly. 'I'll soon be in a sweat, just keeping up with you.'

'We're not going any farther, anyway,' the widow replied, stopping to get her breath back. 'You can see the woods now, which is where we usually keep the cattle in the summer – when they're not out on the islands, that is.'

Carlsson cast a knowledgeable eye over the woods and saw at once that there was quality timber growing there as well as many loads of firewood.

'But my, oh my, oh my, what an unbelievable mess. Everything's such a tangle of brushwood and toppings that not even a tink or a gipsy could fight his way through it!'

'Right, Carlsson, you can see for yourself the state of things, and it's about time someone took charge and dealt with it all. You strike me as just the man to set it to rights. Am I right, Carlsson?'

'Yes, yes, I'll certainly pull my weight if the others pull theirs – but you'll have to back me up,' Carlsson said uneasily, knowing in his heart it was not going to be the easiest thing in the world to secure his status as corporal when the rank and file had been holding the fort for so long.

They walked home, endlessly discussing how Carlsson could gain and retain the supremacy which he persuaded her was the essential condition for the farm to flourish. By now it was time for the Sunday service but there was no sign of any of the men. As usual when it was time to hear the Word of God, the two hunters had gone off to the woods with their guns and Rundqvist had found some sunny spot to hide in. Carlsson assured the widow they could dispense with a congregation, pointing out that if they opened the kitchen door the girls could also receive some nourishment from the Word while the pots were boiling. And when the old woman expressed her concern that she would be unable to read the Word, Carlsson was immediately ready to take over the duty.

'Oh yes, indeed yes!' He had officiated at so many services during his time at the Procurator-Fiscal's that nothing could go wrong.

The widow took out the almanac and looked up the text for the day which, this being the second Sunday after Easter, turned out to be the parable of the Good Shepherd. Carlsson took Luther's *Homily Book* from the shelf and sat on a chair in the middle of the floor, a position which – in his imagination – allowed the whole congregation to see him properly. Then he opened the book and began first to deliver the day's text in a loud voice, running up and down the expressive scale as he had heard itinerant preachers doing and, indeed, had done himself.

'At that time Jesus said unto the Jews: I am the good shepherd: the good shepherd giveth his life for the sheep. But he that is an hireling, and not the shepherd, whose own the sheep are not, seeth the wolf coming, and leaveth the sheep, and fleeth.'

A strange sense of personal responsibility came over Carlsson as he uttered the words 'I am the good shepherd', and he looked out of the window meaningfully as if seeking Rundqvist and Norman, the fugitive hirelings.

The old woman nodded in sorrowful agreement and took the cat up on her lap as if she were opening her bosom to the lost sheep.

Carlsson read on in a voice trembling with emotion, as though he had written it himself.

'But he that is an hireling fleeth – yes, he fleeth!' he began to embroider the theme. 'Because he is an hireling and careth not for the sheep,' he roared.

27

'I am the good shepherd, and know my sheep, and am known of mine,' he continued by heart as if it were a quotation from the catechism. Then he dropped his voice and lowered his eyes, seemingly affected by deep sorrow at the wickedness of mankind. With strong emphasis, sideways glances and a touch of sly insinuation, he whispered, as though he found it painful to have to denounce certain nameless rogues and had no desire to accuse them openly.

'And other sheep I have, which are not of this fold: them also must I bring, and they shall hear my voice!' And then prophetically, full of hope and confidence, Carlsson's face was transfigured by a smile and he whispered: 'And there shall be one fold, and one shepherd.'

'And one shepherd!' the old woman echoed, her thoughts going in a very different direction to Carlsson's.

Then he began to read from the homily book. He made a quick estimate of the number of pages, grimaced when he saw it was 'a hell of a long bit', but plucked up courage and started. The exposition of the theme tended to steer clear of Carlsson's concerns, concentrating more on a Christian symbolic interpretation, for which reason Carlsson's attention was less engaged than it had been by the text itself. He rushed through column after column at a frenetic pace, speeding up even more when it was time to turn the pages in the hope of being able to lick his thumb and turn two pages at once without Madame Flod noticing.

Realising he was nearing the end and suspecting he was about to collide with an Amen, Carlsson eased off the pace. Too late – he had licked his thumb too thoroughly and as a result he turned over three pages at once, bumping into an Amen right at the top of the page, just as if he had banged his head against a wall. The widow was jolted awake and, still in a daze, looked at the clock, which caused Carlsson to repeat the Amen, garnishing it a little with 'in the name of the Father, the Son and the Holy Ghost, and for the sake of Jesus Christ, Our Saviour'.

To round things off and atone for the parts he had omitted, he recited the Lord's Prayer so slowly and in such moving tones that the widow, who was sitting in the full glare of the sun, nodded off again but managed to rouse herself just as Carlsson, to obviate the need for awkward explanations, put his face down into his left hand in order to offer up a silent prayer that it would have been improper of her to interrupt.

Madame Flod, who was also feeling a bit guilty, tried to show she had been paying attention by expressing in her own words what she had learnt, but Carlsson cut her short with an unconditional statement that, according to the fundamental text and the words of Our Saviour himself, there could be no more than *one* fold and *one* shepherd! Only *one*, *one* for all, *one*, *one*, *one*!

At that moment Clara yelled for them all to come for dinner. From the depths of the wood two happy shouts – accompanied by gunshots – responded to her call, while from the smithy chimney, as if from a hungry belly, rose Rundqvist's unmistakeable and more original 'Poo-ee!'

Soon the lost sheep could all be seen trotting towards the cooking pot, where the old woman received them with mild reproaches for their absence from the service. None of these innocents was short of an excuse, all of them insisting they had not heard anyone calling for them – otherwise they would have come *at once*.

Carlsson comported himself with Sabbath decorum at the dinner table whereas Rundqvist rambled on obscurely about the 'strrordinary pecoolier' developments in agriculture, from which Carlsson realised he had already been formally enrolled in the opposition.

After dinner, at which the main dish consisted of a couple of eider duck boiled in milk and peppercorns, the men went off to separate rooms for a snooze, but Carlsson took his hymn book from his chest and sat on a dry rock outside, turned his back to the window and had a nap, which the old woman thought augured well as a way of spending an otherwise wasted Sunday afternoon.

When Carlsson thought enough time had elapsed to make his devotions convincing, he rose, went into the cottage without knocking and came straight out with his desire to see his room. The widow tried to delay things, making excuses about needing to clean it and so on, but Carlsson stood his ground until she took him up to the attic. Right under the roof-trusses there was a small square box-room with wooden walls and a small window in the gable end, hidden at present behind a blue-striped roller-blind. The room contained a bed and a small table in front of the window with a water-jug standing on it. There were things hanging up all round the walls and, although covered by white sheets, they appeared to be articles of clothing – which, indeed, is what they proved to be since a coat collar stuck up here and a trouser leg hung down there. Underneath stood a whole rack of shoes, men's and women's all jumbled together, and over by the door stood a massive iron-bound chest with a chased copper key-plate.

Carlsson pulled up the blind and opened the window to let out the smell of damp, camphor, pepper and wormwood. He put his cap down on the table and declared he would sleep soundly in this room. In response to Madame Flod's fears that the cold would disturb his sleep, he confessed to preferring to sleep in the cold, something that would be out of the question in the heat of the kitchen.

The widow thought things were moving too quickly and wanted to remove the clothes first so they would not pick up the smell of tobacco, but Carlsson promised not to smoke and assured her several times they could stay: he wouldn't as much as look at them and certainly didn't want to put her to any trouble for his sake. He would slip into bed quietly at night, empty his own pot and make the bed in the morning. No one else even needed to put their head round the door since he recognised that Madame Flod was concerned about her belongings – and there certainly seemed to be a hell of a lot of valuable stuff.

Once he had talked the old woman round, Carlsson went downstairs, lugged up his trunk and schnapps bottle, hung his jersey on a nail by the window and placed his sea-boots with the other pairs of shoes.

Then he requested a conversation at which Gusten must be present, since it was time to divide up the jobs and assign every man his duties.

They had some difficulty in locating Gusten and prevailing on him to stay in the parlour for a while. Even then he took no part in the negotiations, merely answering every question with an objection and raising difficulties. In short, he was against everything.

Carlsson tried to win him over with flattery, to crush him with superior knowledge, to appeal to his respect for the wisdom of his elders, but it was all water off a duck's back. Finally both sides grew weary of it and before they knew it Gusten had simply disappeared.

It was evening by now and the sun was sinking down into a misty haze that then began to rise and fill the sky with small feathery clouds. The air was still warm and Carlsson, with no particular aim in mind, strolled down the meadow and into the ox-paddock. The hazel bushes were in flower, though you could still see through them, and he wandered along the tunnel they made over a sunken path that led down to the beach at the spot usually used for loading firewood onto the merchant's sloop.

Suddenly he stopped and through the juniper bushes he caught sight of Gusten and Norman up on a slab of rock in an open glade, peering in all directions, guns fully cocked and at the ready.

'Quiet, he's coming!' Gusten whispered loud enough for Carlsson to hear. Assuming they meant him, Carlsson immediately hid in the bushes.

Then, over the young spruce trees, a bird came flying along, slowly and heavily like an owl, its wings drooping. A second bird followed right behind it.

'*Orrrt-orrrt tsiwick*,' their calls sounded in the air above, followed by *bang! bang!* as both guns spat plumes of smoke and pellets.

The branches of a birch tree cracked and rustled as a woodcock came spinning down no more than a stone's throw from Carlsson.

The hunters ran to pick up their prize, which provided them with an excuse for a short exchange of views.

'That one got what was coming to it!' Norman said, ruffling the breast feathers of the still warm bird.

'I know someone else who ought to get what's coming to him!' Gusten said, his thoughts on other things in spite of the excitement of the hunt. 'See that sod! Now he's getting to sleep in the attic!'

'No, he can't be!' Norman said to encourage him further.

'He bloody is! And he's going to put the farm in order. As if we didn't know better than him! But that's the way of it, new brooms sweep best – while they're still new, anyway. But if he tries it on with me, he'll soon see! I'm not the man to stand aside just because he's in a bloody hurry. Just let him try and he'll find out how hard life can be! Shush now, the other one's coming back.'

The hunters reloaded and ran back to their positions, but Carlsson crept quietly home, determined to go on the offensive the moment he had made the necessary preparations.

When he went up to his attic that evening he pulled down the blind and lit a candle. Being alone he felt rather low at first and he felt, too, the onset of some trepidation about the people he was cutting himself off from. In the past he had always been one of the flock, day and night, always prepared to be spoken to, always having someone there to listen when he wanted to chat. But now it was silent, so silent that – out of habit – he was waiting to be spoken to and imagining he was hearing voices where there were none. His mind, accustomed to spilling out all its thoughts in speech, began to fill with an unused surplus of thoughts that germinated and sprouted and wanted to burst forth in any form at all; they made him feel so ill at ease that restful slumber evaded him.

He began walking back and forth in his stockinged feet, back and forth between the window and the door of his small room, concentrating all his attention on the work of the coming day. He organised the tasks in his head, allotted them, met the objections in advance, overcame obstacles and, after an hour's work, his mind was at rest. He felt his head was in proper order, lined and ruled like an account book in which all the entries have been put in their proper place and totalled up so that the current balance is apparent at a glance.

Then he went to bed and, alone between the fresh clean sheets, with no fears that anyone would come and disturb him during the night, he began to feel more independent, more of his own man; he was like a runner on a plant, growing out and putting down its own roots, ready to be separated from its parent bush, to live its own life and fight its own battles – which will almost certainly call for more effort but will also bring more satisfaction.

So he fell asleep, ready to face life's Monday and the working week.

CHAPTER III

*The farm-hand plays his trump-card, rules the roost and pushes
the young cockerels off the perch.*

The bream spawned, the juniper shed its pollen, the bird-cherry flowered and Carlsson sowed spring rye over the frosted autumn-sown grain, slaughtered six cows and bought dry hay for the rest so that they could get back on their feet and be let out into the woods. He did the work of two, fitting things out and setting everything to rights, and he had a way of getting the other hands to put their shoulders to the wheel that brooked no resistance.

Born of somewhat indeterminate parentage at an iron-works in Värmland, he had shown a distinct distaste for physical work ever since his childhood, indeed, he had shown quite incredible ingenuity in finding ways of avoiding this tiresome consequence of 'the Fall of Man'.

Along with that, he was driven by a desire to see and experience every aspect of human activity, with the result that he did not stay in any one place longer than was necessary to acquire what he wanted before moving on to some new field of work. After being a blacksmith he had moved on to farm-work, then tried life as a stable-man before working in a shop, after which he had become a garden labourer, navvy, brickmaker and finally pedlar of religious tracts. As a result of all these moves he had developed a degree of versatility, along with a talent for adapting to any situation and to all kinds of people: he could recognise their intentions, read their thoughts and guess their secret desires. He was, in short, a man whose talents elevated him above his surroundings and his range of skills made him more fitted to command and lead than to obey those inferior to him – his rightful place was riding on the cart rather than being one of its wheels.

Chance alone had thrown Carlsson into his new position but he saw at once that he could be useful in it, that he had the necessary skills to make this unprofitable farm profitable and thereby quickly win approval and, indeed, finally become indispensable. He now had a definite goal and the force that drove him was the hope – indeed, the certainty – that his efforts would be rewarded with an even better position. He was, quite obviously and indisputably, working for the others, but he was ensuring his own prosperity at the same time and, if he could make it appear he was devoting all his time and effort for their benefit, he would prove himself a good deal smarter than all the people who would have liked to be in the same position but lacked the ability.

Gusten, the son, was the main obstacle in Carlsson's way. He had that distinct taste for the unpredicatable and for the unexpected that characterises hunters and fishermen; he also had a marked aversion to order and certainty. Cultivating the land, in his view, could never yield more than you had expected – never any more and, more often than not, much less. On the other hand, if you trawled or put out nets you might get nothing on one occasion but a dozen times more than you had reckoned with on another. If you went out shooting long-tailed duck you might sometimes bag a seal. If you had spent half the day hiding out among the skerries for merganser you might suddenly find that you had eider in your sights. There was always something and it was often something other than you had expected. Hunting, moreover, being a superior right passed down by the upper classes, was still considered to be grander and more dignified than trudging along behind the plough or the dung-cart. This perception was so deep-rooted among the common people that there were even some farm-labourers who were not prepared to drive a pair of oxen, possibly because oxen have been neutered, or perhaps because horses have been held in such superstitious respect

35

since times of old.

Rundqvist was another stumbling block. He was actually a cunning old rogue, who was trying in his own way to engineer a return to a Garden of Eden in which he would be liberated from hard labour and given ample opportunity for long midday naps and large drams. Partly by claiming knowledge of hidden mysteries, partly by his way of laughing off everything serious – particularly heavy work – and partly also, when the worst came to the worst, by pretending to mental and physical infirmity, he had worked out how to attract the sympathy of his fellows, especially when that sympathy expressed itself in the form of a cup of coffee with a dash of schnapps or half a pound of snuff. He knew how to geld sheep and pigs and reckoned he could locate springs with a divining-rod. He also claimed to have ways of attracting perch into the nets and to be able to cure all sorts of minor ailments in other people, though he kept quiet about his own. If it had been raining for half the month he would forecast good weather at the new moon, and he was not averse to making offerings of money – other people's – under a large rock on the sea-shore to ensure the arrival of the herring. He knew some malicious tricks too, or so he said, such as how to make penny-cress flourish in a neighbour's field, how to make cows run dry or people and animals ill. Spells such as these meant that people regarded him with some measure of fear and preferred to stay on the right side of him.

The merits he did possess, such as they were, and which had made him indispensable, were that he was both a blacksmith and a carpenter; but what really made him a dangerous rival for Carlsson was his incredible knack of doing things that were clearly visible, whereas whatever Carlsson might do under the roof of the byre or out in the fields was much less eye-catching.

Then there was Norman, a good enough worker, whom Carlsson needed to wean away from the powerful influence of Gusten and win back to the regular work of the farm.

Carlsson had his work cut out, then, and it took no small degree of diplomatic skill for him to get his own way but, being smarter than they were, he won.

He avoided entering into open hostilities with Gusten and left him alone once he had coaxed his ally Norman away with various inducements. Which did not prove difficult to achieve since Gusten, to be honest, was pretty mean and had almost always treated Norman as no more than the oarsman on their hunting trips, never allowing him to take the first shot at anything. If Norman was given a dram, you could be sure Gusten would have three on the quiet, so the benefits Carlsson now provided – more pay, a pair of socks, a shirt and some small extras – along with Carlsson's growing influence, which held out more promise than Gusten's waning power, quickly led to Norman's defection. This, in turn, rather dampened Gusten's enthusiasm for hunting since going out in the boat alone was not much fun and so, for lack of other company, Gusten joined the others in work on the farm.

Rundqvist, on the other hand, was a slippery old eel and getting him to take the bait was rather more difficult, but Carlsson hooked him soon enough. Instead of spending money Carlsson had the sweep-nets mended, replacing all the warp-lines and, lo and behold, more herring were caught than before. Instead of using a divining-rod cut from parasitic rowan to dowse for new wells, he had the old well cleaned out and re-lined, built a wall round it and fitted a pump. And so the divining-rod ended up on the rubbish heap. Instead of muttering incantations and passing flame across the cows' backs, he had them groomed and put down dry straw for them. Rundqvist might be able to forge iron horseshoe nails but Carlsson could make wire nails; Rundqvist could carve a rake but Carlsson could make both wooden ploughs and clod-crushers.

When Rundqvist realised he was being ferreted out of his burrow and pushed aside, he resorted to more conspicuous activities like tidying up round the cottage, clearing away the junk people had 'accidentally' dropped on the ground through laziness or in the winter darkness, fussing about the hens and the cat, and fitting a new latch on the door.

'Isn't that kind of Rundqvist,' Carlsson heard the girls in the kitchen say. 'He's a nice enough old fellow, whatever they say.'

But Carlsson was quick off the mark. One morning the stove had been painted white; another day the water buckets had been painted green, with black rings and white hearts; yet another day the firewood had all been stacked under a roof he had built behind the storehouse. Carlsson had learnt from his enemy the value of winning over those who ruled in the kitchen – and the new pump made him invincible.

Rundqvist, however, was both stubborn and wily and one Saturday night he painted the outside privy a glaring red. Carlsson immediately got hold of Norman, bribed him with a couple of gills of schnapps and on the eve of Trinity Sunday Madame Flod could hear tiptoeing and creeping round the walls of the house but, since she was too sleepy to get up, it was morning before she saw that the whole house was a fiery red with white window-frames and sill flashings. This marked the end of the campaign which, given Rundqvist's age, was proving far too strenuous for him. Everyone was laughing at his peculiar choice of the privy as the place to start doing up the farm and Norman, true turn-coat that he was, made up a joke that did the rounds for a long time. It went something like this: 'Always start from the bottom, said Rundqvist when he painted the privy!' So Rundqvist gave in, but was always on the watch either for new bits of mischief he could get up to or for the chance of a favourable truce.

Gusten let them get on with it. He just watched and thought it all augured well: 'You do the ploughing,' he thought, 'and I'll gather the harvest.'

There had not, however, yet been time for Carlsson's activities to reap any tangible profit. The money brought in by selling the cows had lain in the bureau for a few days, making a good impression, but it had soon flowed out again, its absence leaving a sense of loss behind it.

Midsummer was approaching and Carlsson had had plenty to do and little time for strolling round. But one Sunday afternoon when he was walking round the farm his eye was caught by the big farmhouse standing there empty with its blinds drawn down. Being nosy by nature he went over and tried the door. It was unlocked. He went into the hall and then to the kitchen. Moving on he entered a large room with the feel of a gentleman's residence to it. It had white curtains, an Empire sofa-bed with brass decorations, and a mirror with a carved, gilded frame and glass with bevelled facets. He could see immediately how grand it all was – the sofa, the bureau and the tiled stove – all exactly as in a manor house. On the other side of the hallway was another room, just as big and containing an open fireplace, a dining table, sofas and a wall-clock. He was filled with amazement and respect, feelings that quickly turned to pity and scorn for the owners' lack of enterprise when he saw that the house also possessed two bedrooms with several beds already made-up.

'Oh dearie, dearie me,' he thought aloud, 'so many beds and not a summer guest in sight!'

Excited by the thought of this future source of income Carlsson went back to Madame Flod and lectured her on the wastefulness of not renting the house to summer visitors.

'Bless my soul, we'd never find anyone who'd want to come here,' the widow said nervously.

'But how do you know? Have you ever tried to rent it out? Have you ever advertised it?'

'We might just as well throw our money in the sea,' she said.

'Well, we throw our nets into the sea, don't we?' Carlsson answered. 'We have to if we want to catch anything.'

'You can try if you want to, but we won't get any visitors here,' the old woman said, having long since ceased to believe her wishes would be fulfilled.

A week later an elegant gentleman came walking across the meadow, looking all round. He approached closer and the only one to greet him to the farm was the dog, the rest of the inhabitants – whether from habit, shyness or good manners – having hidden in the kitchen or the parlour after first clustering outside to gape at the stranger. Not until the gentleman reached the door did Carlsson, the most courageous of them, step out to meet him.

The visitor had read an advertisement...Yes, indeed, this is the place! He was shown up to the farmhouse and he was really taken with it. Carlsson had promised any necessary improvements, anything, as long as 'Sir' would make up his mind straight away since there had, of course, been many expressions of interest and the season was well advanced. The stranger, who seemed enchanted by the beauties of the spot, made up his mind quickly and, after various intimate questions from both parties about financial matters and family circumstances, the gentleman departed.

Carlsson accompanied him to the gate and then rushed back to the cottage where he laid out seven Bank of Sweden ten krona notes plus one five krona note from a private bank.

'It's dreadful to take so much money off people,' Madame Flod murmured.

Gusten, however, thought it was all to the good and, for the first time ever, praised Carlsson in public when the latter told them how he had squeezed the gentleman with the hint of many others being interested.

Money on the table, that was Carlsson's trump card and he could speak with more authority after this event, in which his experience of commerce had come in so handy. It was not only the ready money from the rent they would be getting either, indirect benefits would now pour in and Carlsson was not slow to describe them to his listeners.

They would be able to sell their fish, milk, eggs and butter; nor would the visitors be getting their firewood for nothing – not to mention errands to Dalarö at a krona a time; and they might even be able to sell a calf, a sheep, a hen that had stopped laying, potatoes and vegetables. And so on, and so on ... there was so much money to be made ... and he really was a gentleman, that fellow.

The golden geese arrived on Midsummer's Eve, in the form of a family consisting of the gentleman himself, his wife, a sixteen-year-old daughter, a six-year-old son and two maids. The gentleman was a violinist in the court orchestra, a peaceable sort of fellow in his early forties, and in good circumstances. He was German by birth and had some little trouble understanding the islanders: he therefore limited himself to nodding agreement and saying 'wunderbar' to everything that was said, with the result that he quickly gained the reputation of being a very nice gentleman. His wife was a respectable woman who took proper care of the house and of her children and whose dignified manner inspired obedience in her maids without her having to resort either to rage or to bribery.

Carlsson, as the least shy and most talkative of the locals, immediately took charge of the visitors. He also felt he had some sort of prior claim on them since he was the one who had brought them here, and none of the other islanders had either the initiative or the social talents to dispute his position. The arrival of these townspeople, however, could not fail to have an impact on the minds and habits of the islanders. To see – on a daily basis – people going round in their best clothes, treating every day as if it were Sunday, rowing without having anywhere in particular to go, fishing without caring about the fish, bathing, making music, passing the time as if there were no cares nor duties in the world – none of this caused envy at the start, rather a sense of wonder that life could be like that and admiration for people who could arrange such a pleasant, calm, pure and, above all, genteel existence for themselves without anyone being able to accuse them of having harmed anyone or of exploiting the poor. Gradually and imperceptibly the people of Hemsö began to dream their own quiet dreams, to cast long, stealthy glances up at the big farmhouse. If they caught a glimpse of a bright summer frock in the meadow, they would stop and stand, enjoying the sight as if gazing at some object of beauty; if, through the branches of the trees, they caught sight of a white veil decorating an Italian straw hat or a red silk ribbon adorning a slim waist out in a boat in the bay, they would fall silent, filled with devout longing for something they did not know, did not dare hope for, but which they were nevertheless drawn to.

The conversations and the hurly-burly in the kitchen and

the old cottage took on a more tranquil tone. Carlsson was never to be seen except in a clean white shirt and he took to wearing a blue cap, bit by bit easing himself into the role of factor. He had a pencil in his breast pocket or behind his ear and he would often smoke a small cigar.

Gusten, by contrast, withdrew, keeping his distance so as not to suffer by comparison. He would talk bitterly about city folk in general and he frequently felt the need to remind both himself and the others about the money they now had in the bank. And he began to take long detours to avoid passing the big house and all those light frocks.

Rundqvist went round with a glowering face and spent most of the time in the smithy, announcing he couldn't give a damn about any of them – and still wouldn't even if one of them had been the Queen Mother in person. Norman began wearing his army cap again and buckling his belt over his jersey; he took to prowling round the pump, where the visitors' maids came every morning and evening.

Worst affected, however, were Clara and Lotten, who had to watch their menfolk deserting them and disloyally transferring their attentions to the visitors' maids. The latter received letters addressed to 'Miss' and wore hats when they went to Dalarö, whereas Clara and Lotten went round barefoot since the muck in the byre would have quickly ruined their boots and it was too warm to wear shoes either in the meadow or in the kitchen. They had no choice but to wear dark dresses and what with sweat and soot and chaff they could not even get away with a bit of white edging; Clara tried wearing some cuffs but they ended up in a mess and when the others noticed she became the butt of their prolonged mirth for trying to compete. On Sundays, however, Clara and Lotten got their own back when, simply in order to wear their best clothes, they demonstrated a regularity in churchgoing they had not shown for years.

Carlsson was forever finding excuses to visit the professor. He would always stop at the porch if anyone was sitting there and ask how they were, forecast good weather, suggest excursions and give advice and information about the fishing.

Now and then he would be given a glass of beer or a brandy and the others soon began to mutter that he only went there to sponge on the visitors.

One Saturday when the visitors' cook was due to go over to Dalarö to do the shopping there was some discussion as to who should take her. Carlsson simply decided the matter to his own advantage since the little maid with her pale complexion and black hair had made a profound impression on him. When Madame Flod objected that Carlsson, as the manager and most important man on the farm, should not be running small errands, Carlsson replied that the professor had expressly asked for him since there were important letters in the post. Contrary to his usual attitude, Gusten seemed rather keen on doing the job and suggested he could easily take charge of the letters, but Carlsson stated emphatically that there was no question of him allowing the 'farmer himself' to perform the sort of menial task that would make people gossip. So that was the situation.

A trip to Dalarö was not without its perks, as the quick-witted farm-hand had recognised from the start. Firstly, there was the pleasure of accompanying the girl in the boat, with the chance to indulge in some undisturbed banter and joking. Then, no doubt, both food and gratuities would be in evidence. It would also give Carlsson the chance to get on the right side of the Dalarö merchants by introducing a new customer, and that always resulted in some small gestures of gratitude – a dram here, a cigar there. On top of which, dressed in his Sunday best and in the company of a young lady from Stockholm, he could bask in the reflected prestige that came from executing a commission on behalf of the professor.

As these trips to Dalarö only happened once a week they did not disrupt the regular work of the farm in any way and Carlsson was smart enough to give the men set quotas of work to be achieved on the days he was away – so and so many yards of ditching, so and so many strips of ploughing, so and so many trees to be felled, after which they were free. And they were happy to go along with this because it meant they could have the evening off even though it was a week-day. It was at times such as these, when measuring out the work to be done and later inspecting the completed jobs, that Carlsson's pencil and newly-acquired notebook really came into their own. He was becoming more and more accustomed to acting the factor and moving the actual work onto the shoulders of the others. By this time, too, he had done out his attic bedroom as a bachelor's private room. He had started smoking in it some time before but now, on the table by the window, he laid out a green pocket ink-well, a pen-holder, a pencil, several sheets of notepaper, a candlestick and a matchbox stand so that the whole arrangement looked like a desk. The window looked out at the big farmhouse and he sat there in his leisure hours watching the comings and goings of the distinguished visitors and even providing them with demonstrations of his ability to write. In the evening he would open the window, rest his elbow on the sill and sit there reading a magazine while puffing at his pipe or a cigar stump he had dug out of his waistcoat pocket. Seen from below it looked as if it was the master of the farm sitting up there.

But when dusk fell and he had lighted the candle, he would lie down on his bed and smoke. That was when his dreams came – or plans, rather; they were dependent on circumstances that had not yet arisen but which, with just a little polishing, might possibly be turned into reality.

As he lay on his back one evening, puffing out clouds of Black Anchor to ward off the mosquitoes, his eye came to rest on the white sheet hanging over Old Flod's clothes at the very moment the sheet slipped and fell to the floor. He saw the whole of the late farmer's wardrobe file past like a shadowy column of soldiers, first marching to the window and then back to the door in the light of the candle flickering in the draught. He imagined he saw the deceased in all the guises represented by the clothes hanging there in front of the patterned wallpaper. There he was in his blue serge jacket and grey corduroy trousers with baggy knees, sitting at the rudder of his boat as he sailed to town with fish and then, after the sale, drinking toddy with the fish-merchant at the Mässingsstången tavern down in Stadsgården. Next he appeared in the black frock-coat and long, baggy, black trousers he wore to church for communion or for weddings, funerals and christenings. Then came the black sheepskin jacket he wore when he stood on the shore, heaving on the drag-net in autumn and spring. Next, taking pride of place, was his great sealskin coat, which still bore the stains from the Christmas party when the last thing he drank in this coat was mulled wine. And there, too, hung the long sash used to fasten it, embroidered with green, red and yellow woollen thread; like some great sea serpent the sash coiled right down to the floor and hid its head in the leg of a boot.

Carlsson felt warm all over as he imagined himself wearing that beautiful, silky fur-coat, saw himself in a seal-skin hat with ring-shaped markings, flying across the ice in a sledge to visit neighbours, who would be welcoming their Christmas guests with fires on the shore and gun-shots. He would throw off his outer garments in the warmth of their cottage and stand there in his black frock-coat to be greeted in familiar terms by the pastor. Then he would sit in state at the head of the table while the farm-hands clustered in the door-way or clambered up on the window-sill.

These images of the bliss he so desired became so real that he leapt to his feet and before he knew it had slipped into the fur-coat and was standing there in the middle of the floor stroking the cuffs. His whole body rejoiced at the feel of the collar tickling his cheek. Then he put on and buttoned up the black frock-coat, placed his shaving mirror on a chair and looked to see how the coat sat at the back. He slid his hand in under the lapel and walked backwards and forwards across the room. The silky smooth cloth gave off a feeling of wealth, of ample plenteousness, as he carefully parted the tails of the coat and sat down on the edge of the bed, pretending to be out visiting.

As he sat there deep in these intoxicating dreams he heard voices chatting happily outside and when he listened more carefully he heard Ida – she was the pretty cook – and Norman, their voices weaving and twining into one another, almost as if kissing. He felt a sudden pang, quickly put the frock-coat and the fur-coat back on their hangers under the sheet and, arming himself with a new cigar, he went down the stairs.

Being so busy and so exclusively concerned with his serious plans for the future, Carlsson had avoided any dealings with the girls because he knew how time-consuming such involvement could be. He was also well aware that the moment he made any advances on that front he might easily leave himself vulnerable in areas that could be difficult to defend: any reverse in the lists of love would put an end to his authority and his prestige.

But now, with this acknowledged beauty at stake and with the winner having so much to gain, he felt compelled to raise his comb and flash his spurs, determined to make himself cock of the walk. He walked down to the wood-pile, where the dalliance was already under way. It was annoying, he thought, that the competition was only that little runt Norman – pity it hadn't been Gusten at least. Well, he'd show him!

'Good evening, Ida,' he began, pretending not to notice his rival, who unwillingly ceded his place by the fence, which was immediately taken over by Carlsson.

So he opened his game, using his superior fluency and not letting Norman get a word in edgeways, while Ida carried on picking up firewood and sticks for her basket. Ida, however, was as flighty as if the moon was on the turn and continued to throw an occasional word in Norman's direction, but Carlsson caught them in flight and sent them back nicely wrapped and decorated. The pretty cook was enjoying the contest and encouraged Norman to split some sticks for her, but before the lucky fellow had time to go round to the gate Carlsson had stepped over the spiky fence, taken out his clasp-knife, selected a dry spruce-tree and was cutting it up. Within a couple of minutes he had filled the basket with sticks, picked it up with his little finger and carried it right into the kitchen with Ida following him. He took up position by the door-post, with his back spread wide so that no one could go in or out. Norman, who had failed to come up with a plausible task, wandered round the wood-pile a few times in melancholy contemplation of how easy life's path was for those who had enough cheek. He then decamped to the well, where he sat on the wall and squeezed out his lamentations in the form of a schottische on his accordion.

The gentle tones emanating from the metal reeds of the accordion carried through the heavy evening air, passed the guard in the doorway and reached the throne of mercy standing by her stove in the kitchen – reminding Ida that she needed to go to the well to fetch drinking water for the professor. Carlsson went with her but was less sure of himself now that the contest had moved on to ground that was unfamiliar to him. To counter the magical effect of the siren-song, Carlsson took Ida's copper jug and whispered soft sounds in tones as languishing and melodious as he could make them, as if he were trying to put words to the seductive music and thus reduce the accordion solo to a subordinate accompaniment. But just as they reached the well they heard Madame Flod's voice calling from the cottage. She was shouting for Carlsson and from the tone of her voice it was clear that it was urgent. Carlsson's first reaction was anger and he considered not answering her, but the devil got into Norman and he responded with a yell:

'He's here, mistress! He's coming at once!'

Silently damning the treacherous musician to Hell a thousand times over, the victor had to tear himself from the arms of love and leave his half-won quarry to the weaker man, who only had fate to thank for his success as a lover.

Madame Flod shouted again and Carlsson answered angrily that he was coming as fast as he could.

'Come in, Carlsson, come and have coffee and a dram,' she greeted him in the porch, shading her eyes with her hand and peering into the soft summer twilight to see whether he was alone.

In any other circumstances Carlsson would have been glad of her offer but at this moment coffee and schnapps were the last things on his mind. But it was impossible to refuse. To the accompaniment of the victorious and mocking sounds of

Norman playing the Norrköping Sharpshooters' March down by the well in the meadow, he had to go into the cottage. The widow was more mellow than usual and Carlsson found her older and uglier than usual. The more amiable she became, the more brusquely he responded, and the result was that she ended up being almost affectionate.

'Now then, Carlsson,' she finally began as she poured the coffee, 'it's time to invite people for the haymaking next week and, of course, I wanted to talk to you first.'

At this point the accordion fell silent half way through the mellifluous chords of a trio and Carlsson became tense and inattentive before spluttering out a string of dull and rather incoherent words:

'Mm, uh, well, haymaking ... next week.'

'On Saturday I want you to go round inviting people. Take Clara with you. Anyway, I want you to get out a bit too, meet people, show yourself around – that's always good.'

'Ah, but I can't go on Saturday,' Carlsson replied quickly. 'That's when I go to Dalarö for the professor.'

'I'm sure Norman can do that trip for once,' the widow said, turning her back on Carlsson to avoid seeing the look on his face.

At that very moment the soft phrases of the accordion were interrupted by several pauses, its tones fading and slipping away into the summer night, where the spinning-wheel churring of the nightjar could already be heard.

Carlsson broke out in a cold sweat and forced down his coffee and schnapps. He felt as if a heavy rock was pressing down on his chest, his mind was in a daze and all his senses were drained of strength.

'But Norman can't,' he objected. 'Norman can't deal with the professor's business, he's not ... he's not ... authorised!'

'I've already asked the professor,' the old woman said, cutting in, 'and he said he didn't have anything for Saturday.'

Carlsson was devastated. She had cornered him like a mouse and he had no hole to run to.

With his mind at sixes and sevens he was in no condition to

mount a counter-attack, which the old woman recognised and decided to carry on kneading the dough while it was still rising.

'Listen to me now, Carlsson,' she said, 'and don't take offence at what I say because I mean well.'

'You can say what the devil you like, missus, because it's all the same to me now!' Carlsson exclaimed, listening to the ever more poignant notes of the accordion receding to the far end of the meadow and growing fainter.

'All I want to say to you is this, Carlsson: you should think better of yourself than to fool around with the girls. It just leads to trouble in the end, I know that, I certainly do. And I'm telling you with the best of intentions. These town girls always have to have a string of men running after them and they're forever dillying here and dallying there – if they go to the woods with one, they'll be off to the meadow with the next one. And when it all goes amiss they pick the one it's most worthwhile to blame it on. That's the way it goes!'

'I don't give a damn what the boys get up to!'

'Now, now, don't take it to heart so,' Madame Flod comforted him. 'A man like you, Carlsson, should be thinking about marriage rather than running around with skivvies. There are plenty of well-off girls out here in the islands, I can tell you, and if you're smart and watch your step you may come into your own sooner than you think. So don't be stubborn and just listen to what I'm saying to you when I tell you to go round inviting the people in for haymaking. And bear in mind that I wouldn't have asked any old Tom, Dick or Harry to go round on farm business. I've no doubt my son will have something to say about it but I don't care – I'll stick up for the one I choose, you can rest assured of that.'

Carlsson's mood began to grow calmer and he saw the potential benefits to himself of going out as the farm's representative. But he was still too annoyed to be prepared to change tack without having some firmer assurances in advance of agreeing to anything.

'I can't go visiting as I am – I don't have any decent clothes,' he said, dangling his bait.

'Clothes aren't that important,' Madame Flod said, 'but if they are the only things lacking then we can easily find something.'

Carlsson did not want to take things too far along that road and he decided instead to swop her half-promise for a different one: after some to-ing and fro-ing they agreed that Norman would stay at home on Saturday – his presence being essential to the business of sharpening scythes and mending the hay-wain – and Lotten would make the trip to Dalarö.

*

It is three o'clock in the morning of a day in early July. Smoke is already rising from the chimney and the coffee pot is on. The whole house is awake and on the move and out on the grass a long table has already been laid. The haymakers arrived yesterday evening and have slept in the hay-lofts and barns, and twelve tall islanders in white shirt-sleeves and straw hats are now standing in groups outside the cottage, armed with scythes and whetstones. The farmers from Åvassa and Svinnock are there, men already old and with their backs bent from rowing; the Aspön farmer with his massive beard is there, a head taller than all the rest and with the deep, mournful eyes that come from nameless sorrows and uncomplaining solitude in the outermost islands; over there stands the fellow from Fjällång, rugged and knotted like a stunted pine out on the most distant skerry, and there is the man from Fiversätraön, thin, windswept but bright as a piece of dried fish skin; and over there are the famous Kvarnö boat-builders together with the lads from Långviksskär – always the first when it comes to seal-hunting – and the Arnö farmer and his boys. In and among them the girls are flitting round in linen sleeves and head-shawls, dressed in bright cotton dresses with kerchiefs at the bosom; they have brought their own rakes with them, all newly painted in rainbow colours so they look as if they are going to a party rather than to work. The older men give them little pats on the waist and make remarks but the younger ones keep their distance at this time of the morning and wait for evening, twilight, dance and music before playing the games of love. The sun has been up for a quarter of an hour but has still not risen far enough above the fir-trees to warm the dew from the grass. The bay lies smooth as a mirror, framed by pale green reeds from which the cheeping of newly hatched ducklings can be heard among the quacking of the adult ducks. The gulls are fishing for bleak down there, sailing on broad wings as snowy white as the plaster angels in the church. The magpies in the oak-tree by the cellar are awake and chattering and gossiping about all the shirt-sleeved figures they can see round the cottage. Down in the pasture the cuckoo is calling frantically, as if the time for lust will be past once he sees the first haycock. The rasping crex-crex of the corncrake is coming from the rye field and the farm dog is rushing round welcoming old acquaintances. Meanwhile the clatter of cups and dishes, glasses and jugs accompanies the morning repast and shirt-sleeved arms and linen ribbons gleam in the sunlight as they reach across the table to help themselves.

Gusten, though normally shy, was acting as host. Feeling secure among his father's old friends he had pushed Carlsson to one side and was taking charge of the schnapps bottle himself. But Carlsson, who had already made their acquaintance on his visits to invite them, felt quite at home and let himself be treated as an older relation or guest. Being ten years older and looking both mature and manly, it was easy for him to put down Gusten, who could never be more than a boy in the eyes of these men who had been on friendly terms with his father.

Once breakfast was over and the sun higher in the sky, the old soldiers shouldered their scythes and set off down to the big field, followed by the younger men and the crowd of girls.

The hay came up to their thighs and was growing as dense as fur, so Carlsson felt compelled to tell them about the latest methods of cultivating hayfields – how he had cleared away the leaves and last year's grass, levelled out the mole-hills, oversown the frosted patches and watered it all with the run-off from the dung-heap. Then, like a captain, he deployed his forces, assigning the older and wealthier to the places of honour and going last himself, thus ensuring he was not just one of the crowd. And so the haymaking started: two dozen white-sleeved arms in a wedge formation like swans migrating in autumn, scythes heel to heel. Spread out behind them, like a flock of terns swooping and turning hither and thither but still sticking together, came the girls, each following her own mower.

The scythes swished and the dewy hay fell in swathes. All the summer flowers that had dared venture out of the woods and pastures fell side by side: ox-eye daisies and bitter vetch, sticky catchfly and corn gromwell, lady's bedstraw, wild chervil, maiden pinks, field cow-wheat, tufted vetch, butterbur, clover and all the grasses of the meadows. The scents were sweet as honey and spice and the honey bees and bumble bees fled in swarms before the deadly onslaught. Moles crept down into the innards of the earth when they heard the din on their fragile roofs, and a frightened grass-snake hurried down into the ditch and slithered like a sheet-end into a hole. High above the battlefield hovered a pair of pipits whose nest had been trampled under an iron heel, and in the rear came the starlings, tripping along and picking and pecking up all the small bugs now exposed to the glaring sunlight.

The first swathe was cut right up to the headland of the field and there the warriors paused, leaning on the shafts of their scythes to contemplate the devastation they had left behind them, while wiping off the sweat-bands of their caps and taking a fresh pinch of snuff from their brass boxes. The girls behind hurried to catch up with the front line.

And so they are off again, out into the green and flower-bedecked hayfield, which at one moment ripples like water in the rising morning breeze, at the next shows a bright motley of colours as the flowers with stiffer stalks poke their heads above the soft billowing grass, which bows with the wind before settling once more to a smooth green expanse as unbroken as a flat-calm sea.

There is a festive feeling in the air as the men compete at their work: they would sooner drop from sunstroke than lay down their scythes. Carlsson has the professor's cook Ida to do his raking and, since he is at the end of the row, he can show off by turning round and speaking to her without risking a scythe in his calves. But he keeps a stern eye on Norman, who is diagonally in front of him, and whenever Norman tries to cast a moonstruck eye to the south-east he finds Carlsson's scythe swishing at his heels, followed by a warning shout that is more unfriendly than well-meaning: 'You there! Watch out for your hocks there!'

By eight o'clock the meadow is lying there looking like a freshly drilled field, flat as the palm of a hand and with the hay lying in long swathes. Now it is time to inspect the work and judge the quality of the cutting, and Rundqvist is the one on whom judgment falls – everyone can see where he did the cutting since it looks like one fairy ring overlapping the next fairy ring. He defends himself by saying he had been unable to keep his eyes off the girl they had given him, it being some little time since he had a girl running after him.

Then Clara yells for them to come up for breakfast. The schnapps bottle is gleaming in the sun, the bung is out of the barrel of small beer, the pan of potatoes is sizzling on the hearthstone, the herring are steaming on the dish, the butter is out and the bread is cut. Drams are poured and breakfast can begin.

Carlsson basks in the praise he receives and he is exultant. Ida shows him her favour and he is notably assiduous in his attentions to her – but then, she is the beauty of the day. The widow, who is dashing in and out with dishes and plates, often passes the two of them, all too often for Ida not to notice, even though Carlsson does not until Madame Flod gently nudges him in the back with her elbow and whispers:

'Carlsson, you're supposed to be the host here and help Gusten. You're part of this household, you know.'

Carlsson only has eyes and ears for Ida and answers Madame Flod with a jest. But then Lina, the nanny in the professor's household, comes to remind Ida she must go home and do the housework – which causes consternation and sorrow among the men whereas the girls seem only mildly down-hearted.

'How's my raking to be done if I don't have a girl?' Carlsson exclaims, feigning despair to mask his real vexation.

'The mistress will have to do it, then, won't she?' says Rundqvist, who was reputed to have eyes in the back of his head.

'The mistress will have to do the raking,' the men all say in chorus. 'The mistress will have to do it.'

With a shake of her apron the mistress rejects the idea.

'Lord Jesus, you can't expect an old woman like me to go out there with the girls! Not for the world! Not for a moment! You must have taken leave of your senses.'

But her resistance merely encourages them.

'Go on, take the old girl,' Rundqvist whispers, at which Norman brightens up but Gusten's face goes as dark as night.

So there is no choice and, to the accompaniment of noise and laughter, Carlsson rushes into the house to find the widow's own rake, which is somewhere up in the loft. Madame Flod runs after him shouting: 'No, for God's sake, you mustn't go rummaging through my things up there!' And the two of them disappear, followed by loud and pointed remarks from those left behind.

'I think,' Rundqvist says, finally breaking the silence that has arisen, 'I think they're taking their time about it! Norman, go and see what's going on.'

The noisy assent that greets this spurs on Rundqvist who, set on boosting his own importance, continues in the same vein.

'Now what can they be doing up there, I wonder? No, this will never do, I'm getting quite anxious. Does anyone have any idea?'

Gusten went blue in the face as he forced himself to laugh along with the others.

'God forgive my sins,' Rundqvist continued in the same tone. 'I can't bear it any longer. I'll have to go and see for myself what they're up to.'

At that moment, however, Carlsson and the widow come out of the house carrying the rake they have been looking for. And a very fine rake it is, with two hearts and the date 1852 painted on it; Old Flod had made it himself as a gift for his fiancée and it even had dried peas in a knob on the end of the shaft so that they rattled when you shook it. Memories of past pleasures seem to have stirred a sense of happiness in Madame Flod's robust nature and without a trace of unhealthy sentimentality she pointed at the date and said:

'It wasn't yesterday Flod made this rake ...'

'And you climbed into the bridal bed, mistress,' added the farmer from Svinnock.

'Might still climb into another one,' the man from Åvassa said.

'A six-week old piglet and a widow of two years are two things you can't trust,' the fellow from Fjällång teased.

'The drier the kindling, the easier it catches,' the man from Fiversätraön said, raising the stakes.

One by one they took turns in adding fuel to the fire but the old woman just smiled contentedly and dismissed the idea; there was no point in getting cross so she put a good face on it and joined in the merriment.

Then they set off down to the boggy meadow where sedge and Dutch rushes grew as thick as a fir-plantation and the water rose up the legs of the men's boots. The girls, however, took off their shoes and stockings and hung them on the fence.

The widow set to and raked and kept up with Carlsson, her mower, better than the other girls. 'The young couple', as the others called them, quickly became the target of frequent jokes.

Then came dinner-time and soon it was evening. The fiddler had arrived with his fiddle, the barn had been cleared and swept and the worst splinters in the floor stuck down with pitch. When the sun went down, the dancing started.

Carlsson opened the dance with Ida, who was wearing a black dress, cut low and square but with her bosom and neck covered with ruching and a Mary Stuart collar. She stood out as a lady among the farm-girls, awakening their envy and causing some alarm and frostiness among the elderly, but nothing but desire among the boys.

Carlsson was the only one who knew the new waltz so Ida was happy to take him as her partner time after time, especially after a three-step waltz with Norman had gone disastrously wrong, at which the latter – now out of the running – foolishly took it into his head to settle for the accordion as a means of pouring out the pain that was in his heart and making one last effort to trap the gorgeous but inconstant bird he thought he had in his hand some weeks ago but which was now back up on the roof billing and cooing with another. Carlsson, however, found the accordion an unsuitable instrument: he had expressly engaged a real musician and the wheezing accordion really did not go with the nimble fiddle, serving only to disrupt the tempo and bring disorder to the dancing. Seeing a good opportunity to crush his rival, particularly as the general view of the accordion seemed to match his own, Carlsson took a deep breath and yelled across the barn to the unlucky lover, who had retreated to a corner:

'You'm zere, put a sock in that leather wind-bag! If your belly's so full of wind, get outside and squeeze it out!'

Public opinion against the transgressor revealed itself in the broad grins of approval that greeted this suggestion, but Norman had taken a few drinks by this time which, in combination with the ruching at Ida's bosom, endowed him with unexpected courage and made him disinclined to give in.

'You'm zere!' he mimicked Carlsson, who had inadvertently slipped back into his native dialect, which never failed to sound comical to the islanders. 'Coom outside, you'm, and I'll pick the fleas out of your piggy hide!'

Carlsson did not yet consider the situation threatening enough to require fisticuffs and he stuck to the less harmful strategy of bandying abuse.

'Pretty funny pig if it's got fleas on its hide!'

'Must be a Värmland pig, then,' Norman responded.

That struck home at Carlsson's provincial pride and, although he tried to the last to come up with a crushing response, he failed and instead went for his opponent, grabbed him by the waistcoat and dragged him outside.

The girls lined up in the doorway to watch the scrap and it did not occur to anyone to try to intervene.

Norman was small and thick-set but Carlsson was bigger and more heavily-built. In a trice he had thrown off his coat, which he did not want to damage, and the two fighters set to. Norman led with his head, as he had learnt from the pilot lads, but Carlsson caught him, aimed a nasty kick at his groin and Norman collapsed on the dung-heap like a curled-up hedgehog.

'You navvy lout, you!' he yelled, in no condition to continue defending himself with his fists. Carlsson's blood was boiling and, words failing him, he placed his knee on his fallen rival's chest and slapped his cheeks while Norman spat and bit in all directions until a fistful of straw was stuffed into his mouth.

'Now I'll scrub your mug clean for you!' Carlsson said, pulling a bunch of straw out of the dung-heap and rubbing his defeated opponent's face with it until his nose bled. Which unblocked his rival's mouth and allowed Norman, who was foaming with rage, to hurl his whole stock of abuse into the face of the victor, who had no way of restraining the beaten man's tongue.

The music had fallen silent, the dancing stopped and the spectators were commenting on the ins-and-outs of this battle of words and fists, which they were listening to and observing with the same level of unconcern as if it had been a dancing game or a pig being slaughtered – though the older men were of the opinion that Carlsson's onslaught had not, perhaps, been fully in accord with the rules of traditional fighting etiquette. Suddenly, however, there was a scream that caused the group to scatter and which jerked them all out of the festive mood.

'He's pulled a knife!' someone yelled – it was impossible to tell who.

'A knife!' came a voice from the crowd. 'No knives! Get rid of the knife!'

The combatants were surrounded and Norman, who had managed to draw his clasp-knife, was disarmed and set back on his feet once Carlsson had been dragged off him.

'Fighting's one thing, boys, but knives are another,' old Svinnock said, putting an end to the scrap.

Carlsson put on his coat and buttoned it up over his torn waistcoat while Norman went off with one shirt sleeve hanging raggedly down round his leg. Dirty, bloody and with a battered face, he disappeared round the back of the barn rather than let the girls see him in his humiliation.

Carlsson, however, with the happy confidence that comes from being the stronger and victorious one, returned to the dance-floor and, once he had drunk a dram, resumed the wooing of Ida, who received him warmly and with something close to admiration.

Dusk fell and the dancing was going like a threshing machine. Schnapps was flowing freely and less and less attention was being paid to the comings and goings of those present, which is why Carlsson was able to sneak out of the barn with Ida and reach the gate to the paddock without any impertinent questions being asked. But just as the girl had climbed over the stile and he himself was standing on the fence, he heard Madame Flod's voice in the half-darkness, though he could not see her.

'Carlsson? Are you there, Carlsson? Come and have a dance with your hayraker.'

Carlsson did not answer and, instead, crept down and into the paddock as silently as a fox.

The widow had seen him, however, and she had also seen the white neckerchief Ida had tied round her waist to protect her dress from sweaty hands. After calling once more without receiving an answer, she climbed over the stile into the paddock and went after them. The sunken path through the hazel bushes was pitch-black and all she could see was something white moving in the darkness before it finally faded away at the end of the long tunnel. She was about to run after it when she suddenly heard new voices by the stile, a deep voice and a more tinkling one, both of them hushed and, as they came nearer, speaking in a whisper. Gusten and Clara climbed over the fence, which creaked under Gusten's rather unsteady steps, and Clara jumped down, steadied by two strong arms. The old woman hid in the bushes as they passed her, arms round each other's waists, dancing along, half-singing and kissing, just as she too had once danced, sung and kissed. Then the stile creaked again and jumping over it like a bullock came the lad from Kvarnö followed by the girl from Fjällång. Flushed from the dancing and with a smile of abandon that revealed all her white teeth, she stood up straight for a moment right on top of the fence, crossed her raised arms behind her head as if she was going to fall and, with a breathless laugh and flared nostrils, threw herself headlong down into the arms of the boy, who greeted her with a long kiss before carrying her off into the darkness.

The old woman stood behind the hazel bush and watched as couple after couple came, went and came again, just as in her youth, and an old fire began to rekindle beneath the ashes of the past two years.

It was past midnight, the fiddle had eventually fallen silent and the red of the dawn was beginning to show as a faint glow over the woods to the north. The hum of voices in the barn was drowsier and an occasional cheer out in the meadow signalled that the dance was breaking up and the haymakers were preparing for their homeward journeys. She would have to go and bid them farewell. When she reached the sunken path, where the darkness was lifting and the green of the leaves was becoming visible, she caught sight of Carlsson and Ida walking along the top of the bank, hand in hand as if they were about to start dancing a polka. Ashamed of being caught there in the green tunnel, she turned and hurried over the stile to get back before the haymakers set off home. Standing at the other side of the stile, however, was Rundqvist and he clapped his hands when saw her, while she covered her face with her apron to conceal her shame.

'Well, mercy me, if the mistress weren't down in the paddock too! Well, I never – you can't trust the old uns any more than you ...'

She did not listen to the rest and half-ran up to the cottage, where everyone had been looking for her and where she was greeted with resounding cheers, handshakes, thanks for her good hospitality and farewells.

But when all was quiet and those still missing had been called in from the fields and meadows – not all of them, however – the old woman went to bed, where she lay awake for a long time listening to hear whether Carlsson went up the stairs to his attic room.

CHAPTER IV

A wedding is mooted and the widow is taken for her gold.

The hay had been brought in and the rye and wheat harvested. Summer was over and it had been a good one.

'He's got luck on his side, that bugger!' Gusten said about Carlsson, to whom they all attributed their growing prosperity – and not without reason.

The herring had arrived and all the men apart from Carlsson were out in the skerries when the time came for the professor and his family to return to the city for the opening of the opera season.

Carlsson took over their packing and walked round all day with a pencil behind his ear, drinking beer at their kitchen table, at the sideboard in the dining-room or on the bench on the porch. Anything they could not take with them or no longer had any use for passed in his direction: a discarded straw-hat, a pair of worn-out sailing shoes, a pipe, a cigar-holder, unsmoked cigars, empty boxes and empty bottles, fishing rods and empty corned beef cans, corks, sail twine and nails. So many crumbs can fall from a rich man's table that there was a feeling that the professor's family would be missed by everyone; from Carlsson, who was about to lose his sweetheart, all the way down to the hens and pigs, which would no longer enjoy their Sunday dinners from the gentlefolk's kitchen. Clara and Lotten were the least sorry to see the family go since, though they had enjoyed many a cup of good coffee when delivering the milk, they knew the departure of the visitors and the start of autumn would signal the arrival of a new spring for them by removing their serious rivals in the market for love.

As it was the first time a steamer had ever put in there, there was great excitement on the island on the afternoon it arrived to pick up the summer guests. Carlsson took charge of the landing, shouting commands and ranting on as the steamer tried to draw alongside the jetty. In this, however, he was skating on thin ice – too thin to bear his weight – since he knew nothing at all about seamanship. When the rope was thrown and he attempted to give a proud demonstration of his skill in front of Ida and the gentry, the whole coil of rope descended on his head and knocked off his cap, which then fell in the sea. He tried to hang on to the rope while at the same time catching his cap in the air but caught his foot in a coil of rope, performed a staggering dance and fell over to the accompaniment of a storm of invective from the captain and a salvo of jeers from the sailors on the fo'c'sle. Ida turned away, furious at her hero's clumsy antics and close to weeping tears of shame. With a curt farewell she finally left him at the gangway and, when he tried to hold on to her hand and talk about next summer and exchanging addresses and writing letters, the gangway was jerked away under him so that he lurched forward, causing his wet cap to slide to the back of his neck, while the mate roared down at him from the bridge:

'You there, are you ever going to cast off?'

A new shower of opprobrium and abuse hailed down on the unfortunate lover before he managed to cast off the rope. Then the steamer backed down the sound and, like a dog whose master is leaving home, Carlsson ran along the shore, jumping on rocks and stumbling over roots, to reach the headland where he had hidden his gun behind an alder bush in order to fire a salute. But his day was clearly doomed to disaster: as the steamer sailed past and he raised the gun in the air to fire, the shot misfired. Hurling his gun down on the grass, he pulled out his handkerchief, waved it and ran along the shore flapping his blue cotton handkerchief and cheering and panting. There was no response from the boat: not a hand was raised nor a handkerchief waved. Ida had vanished! Indomitable, though furious, Carlsson ran on over boulders, jumped into the water, crashed through alder bushes, came to a fence and leapt halfway through it, scratching himself on the poles. Finally, just as the boat was about to disappear round the headland, he came to a bay full of reeds and, without a second thought, plunged into the water waving his handkerchief yet again and uttering one last despairing hurrah. The stern of the steamer slid away behind the pine-trees and he saw the professor's hat waving good-bye as the ship slipped behind the wooded point, trailing its blue and yellow flag with the posthorn insignia. There was one more glimpse of the flag through the alders and then everything was gone, except for a long cloud of black smoke which hung above the water like a mourning veil and made the sky dark.

Carlsson splashed ashore and plodded step by step back to his gun. He looked at it angrily, as if looking at someone who had let him down, then he shook the pan, put in a new percussion cap and fired a shot without any problem.

Returning to the jetty, he relived the whole sorry performance: he saw himself dancing on the planks of the jetty like a clown at the fairground, heard the laughter and the abuse, remembered Ida's cold, embarrassed look and handshake, could still smell the fumes of coal smoke and engine grease, of fat frying in the galley and of oil-paint on the planking. The steamer had come out here to his growing kingdom and brought with it city folk who scorned him and who in the flicker of an eye had pushed him off the rungs of the ladder up which he had already climbed quite high; moreover – here he felt a lump come to his throat – they had then carried off his summer happiness and his summer joy. For a short while he stared down into the water that the steamer's paddles had churned into a filthy sludge, on the surface of which floated patches of discharged soot and mirrors of oil that glimmered all the colours of the rainbow, like an old window-pane. During its short visit the monster had managed to pollute the clear green water by excreting every kind of filth imaginable – the corks from beer bottles, egg-shells, lemon rind, cigar stubs, spent matches and scraps of paper, all of which the bleak and the gudgeon were now toying with. It was as if the gutters of the whole city had been brought out here only to spew out their abuse and rubbish at one and the same time.

For a moment it all seemed dreadful, and it dawned on him that if he seriously wanted to win his sweetheart he would have to go there, have to move in among the alleys and gutters of the city, where there were high wages and fine clothes, gaslights and shop-windows, where the girl with the ruffle and the cuffs and the button boots was to be found. Everything that tempted him was there. But he hated the city, too, as a place where he was a nobody, a place where they sneered at his dialect, where his coarse hands could not handle the delicate work and where his versatility and many talents would not produce a return. He would nevertheless have to consider it: Ida had said that she would never marry a farm-hand and he had no hope of becoming a farmer. Or had he?

A breeze rose over the sound and a cool wind, gathering in strength, stirred the water so that it began to splash against the piles of the jetty, sweeping away the soot and clearing the bright evening sky. The sighing of the alders, the lapping of the waves and the bumping of the boats jerked him awake and with his gun over his shoulder he walked homewards.

The track led under the hazel bushes and up over a rocky knoll, above which rose a higher wall of grey rock, overgrown with pines; it was a spot he had never visited before.

Driven by curiosity he climbed up through ferns and thickets of raspberry bushes and was soon standing on top of a slab of grey rock on which a sailing beacon had been erected. The island lay spread out below him in the sunset, a panorama of woods and fields, meadows and cottages, encircled by islands and islets and skerries all the way out to the open sea. It was a large piece of this beautiful earth and all of it could be his – the water, the trees and the rocks – if he were to stretch out his hand, just one hand, and withdraw the other hand, the one that was reaching out for vainglory and poverty. He had no need of a tempter at his side bidding him fall to his knees before this picture, rose-tinted by the magical rays of the setting sun:

the blue waters, green woods, yellow fields and red cottages blended into a rainbow capable of bewitching a mind much less receptive than that of the farm-hand.

Angered by the deliberate disregard shown by the faithless Ida, who had managed in no more than five minutes to forget her last little promise to wave good-bye; wounded, as if he had been whipped, by the insults of the arrogant city louts; captivated by the sight of the fertile earth, fish-rich waters and warm cottages – all this led Carlsson to his decision: he would go home, make one last effort (or possibly two) to test the loyalty of her false heart (which may already have forgotten him) and then, short of outright theft, he would help himself to whatever was there for the taking.

*

When he arrived back at the farm and saw the big house standing empty, its curtains taken down and straw and boxes scattered round outside, he felt a lump in his throat as if he had tried to swallow a bite of apple without chewing it. He gathered together his souvenirs of the temporary summer guests in a bag and crept as quietly as possible up to his attic. Once he had hidden his treasures under the bed he sat down at his writing table, took out pen and paper and settled to write a letter. The first page poured out in a broad, unbroken stream of words, partly drawn from the storehouse of his own mind, partly from Afzelius's Swedish chronicles and ballads, which he had read when he was employed by the factor on an estate in Värmland and which had made a strong impression on him.

'Dearest, dearest Friend,' he began, 'I am now sitting alone in my little room and I am missing you something dreadful, Ida. I remember like it was yesterday when you came out here, it was when we was sowing the spring rye and the cuckoo was calling down in the bullock field and now it is autumn and the lads are out in the skerries after herring. I wouldn't be so concerned about it all if you hadn't gone off without waving to me from the steamer which the professor was kind and nice enough to do from the after-deck when he was going round the headland. It's as empty as a hole without you here tonight, Ida, and what makes it worse is that my peace is gone, my heart is heavy. Do you remember, Ida, what you promised not long ago at the haymaking dance, I remember it as if I had written it down, and I can stick by what I promise, which not everybody can. But that doesn't matter and I'm not so particular about what people think about me but I can tell you now that I never forget the person I love.'

The sorrow of parting had now abated somewhat and bitterness raised its head instead, followed in turn by fear of unknown rivals and of the temptations of the city and of Berns' Pleasure Palace. Knowing that he was in no position to prevent the Fall from Grace he feared, he resorted to loftier sentiments: old memories from his days as a hawker of uplifting tracts came to the surface and his tone became elevated, stern and moral – a punishing avenger through whose lips Another (with a capital A!) spoke:

'When I consider how you are now walking alone, Ida, through the city where so many have gone astray, without a steadying hand to turn away the dangers and temptations, when I contemplate all the opportunities for you to skip so lightly along the Broad Road that leads to wickedness and ruin, my heart is sore and I feel I have sinned before God and mankind by leaving you alone in the web of sin. Oh, Ida, I would have been like unto a father to you and you could have turned to old Carlsson as you would turn to a real father ...'

At the words 'father' and 'old Carlsson' his heart softened and he remembered the last funeral he had attended.

'... a father with indulgence and forgiveness in his heart and on his lips. Who knows how long old Carlsson (he had already fallen in love with the words!) will be given in this mortal sphere, who can tell whether the days of his life may be reckoned like unto the drops of water in the sea or the stars in the firmament – or, indeed, whether he will be lying there like dry hay before you know it. And then, perhaps, a certain someone, who does not think so at this moment, will want to raise him from the clay. But let us hope and pray he will be spared to see the day the flowers spring from the earth and the voice of the turtle-dove is heard in the land – which will be a day of delight for many-a-one now sighing and sorrowing and wishing to sing with the psalmist ...'

He had, however, by this point forgotten what it was the psalmist sang and was forced to get up and look for his Bible in the chest. There being over a hundred psalms to choose from, and since Clara was already calling everyone to supper, he had to pick at random and the one he chose was ...

'Thou crownest the year with Thy goodness; and Thy paths drop fatness. They drop upon the pastures of the wilderness: and the little hills rejoice on every side. The pastures are clothed with flocks; the valleys also are covered with corn; they shout for joy, they also sing.'

On reading it through he noted the fortuitous but fortunate allusion to the advantages of the rural life over city life and, since that was precisely the sore point, he decided not to press it but to let a half-sung song speak for the whole.

He began pondering what to write next. He was feeling tired and hungry and there was no way of concealing from himself the fact that, when all was said and done, it made no difference what he wrote – Ida would almost certainly be gone before spring ever returned.

So he signed himself 'Yours truly faithfully and sincerely' and went down to the kitchen for supper. It was already dark and the wind was getting up. Lighting a candle, the widow came and sat down nervously at the table where Carlsson, having lighted a candle, was sitting all alone, while the girls moved quietly and guardedly between the stove and the table.

'You'd better have a dram of schnapps this evening,' Madame Flod said. 'I can see you're in need of one.'

'You're right here,' Carlsson answered, 'it was a fair old job getting all their things on board'.

'There'll be time to rest now, though,' the widow said and went to fetch the hour-glass bottle. 'That's a dreadful wind blowing tonight and it's going round to the east. I wonder how the lads will manage the nets.'

'Look now, I can't do anything about that – I'm not in charge of the weather,' Carlsson snapped. 'But it had better be good next week because I'm planning on taking the fish-cage into town to talk to the fishmonger myself.'

'Really? You're going to do that?'

'Yes, I don't believe the boys are getting a good enough price for the fish – there's something wrong there somewhere, wherever the fault may lie.'

The widow fiddled with the things on the table and felt pretty sure that fish was not Carlsson's only errand in town.

'Mm, and I've no doubt you'll do the polite thing and call on the professor while you're there?'

'Yes, I will if I have time – especially since he has left a bottle basket behind ...'

'Really nice people they were, anyway ... won't you have that dram now, Carlsson?'

'Thank you very much. Yes, they were lovely people, weren't they, and I think they will come again – at least, that's the impression I got from Ida.'

Uttering Ida's name aloud not only gave him great pleasure, it also allowed him to stress the superiority of his position. The widow, on the other hand, recognised the weakness of hers, her inescapable disadvantage, and it brought fire to her eyes and a flush to her cheeks.

'I thought things were over between you and Ida,' the old woman said in a half-whisper.

'Oh Lord no, far from it, far from it,' Carlsson answered, knowing full well that he had something on his hook as he reeled in the line.

'You'll be getting married then?'

'We may well, all in good time. But I'll have to look round for a situation somewhere first.'

The widow's creased face twitched and her thin hand picked and plucked like a feverish patient picking at the sheet.

'So you'll be thinking of leaving us?' she said hesitantly in a dry, tremulous voice.

'It will be time to move on at some point,' Carlsson answered. 'Sooner or later a man wants a place of his own. Nobody wants to wear himself out working for others for no return.'

Clara had come over with the porridge and he felt a sudden desire to tease her.

'Well, Clara, aren't you afraid of the dark, sleeping alone while the boys are away? Would you like me to come down and keep you company?'

'Huh! That won't be necessary!' Clara answered.

There was a moment's silence in the kitchen. The storm outside could be heard roaring through the wood, tearing the leaves off the birches, making the fences shake and battering the weather-vanes and eaves. An occasional gust forced its way down the chimney, blowing fire and smoke out under the hood of the fireplace and making Lotten cover her eyes and mouth with her hand. And when the wind fell for a moment, the waves could be heard pounding on the eastern headland. Suddenly the mongrel started howling outside and then the barking grew more distant as if the dog had run off either to greet or to threaten someone.

'Go and have a look who that might be, will you?' the old woman asked Carlsson, who immediately rose to do so.

Stepping outside the door he could see nothing but darkness so thick it could be cut with a knife and the wind hit him with a gust that made his hair stand up like pea-sticks. He called the dog but the barking was already away over in the meadow by the spring and its note was one of cheerful recognition.

'We've got visitors on their way in spite of the time of night,' Carlsson said to the widow, who had come to the door. 'I wonder who. I'd better go and take a look. Clara, light a lantern and give me my cap!'

He took the lantern and, struggling against the wind out in the field, followed the barks and reached the copse of pines that stood between the meadow and the shore. The barking had stopped but between the sighing and creaking of the trees he could hear the sound of iron-heeled boots clattering on slabby rocks, the crack of branches being snapped as someone tried to find a way through, feet splashing through pools, and a torrent of oaths in answer to the whining dog.

'Hello there! Who's there?' Carlsson shouted.

'The minister!' a husky voice answered. At the same moment Carlsson saw a shower of sparks made by iron heel-plates striking a boulder and a small, stocky man in furs tumbled off a knob of rock and out of the thicket. His face was coarse and weather-bitten, framed by unkempt, grey mutton-chop whiskers and lit up by piercing little eyes beneath eyebrows that sprouted like feather moss.

'What the hell have you got for paths on this island?' he growled by way of greeting.

'Well, Lord Jesus, it's the minister! And out in this foul weather, too!' Carlsson replied respectfully to the oaths with which this curator of souls was greeting him. 'But where is your boat?'

'With the fish cage in it, too, dammit – but Robert's found an anchorage for it. Let's just get inside somewhere – this wind is cutting right through me tonight. Come on, get a move on!'

Carlsson walked in front with the lantern and the minister followed him, followed in turn by the dog, which dashed into the bushes now and again on the scent of a blackcock that had just flown off to the safety of the bog.

The widow, meanwhile, had come outside and was walking towards the approaching lantern. Once she saw that it was the minister, she was pleased to see him and welcomed him in.

He had been on his way to town with his fish when the storm broke and forced him to put ashore for the night. He cursed and swore that he would not get there in time to sell his fish now, since 'every beggar is out here stripping our waters of anything that moves'.

The widow wanted him to come into the parlour but he marched straight into the kitchen to dry out by the fire. The heat and light, however, did not seem to suit him that well and, as he pulled off his greased leather boots, he screwed up his eyes as if he was just waking up. Carlsson helped him off with his sheepskin-lined, grey-green serge coat and soon, clad in a woollen pea-jacket and in stockinged feet, the minister was sitting at the corner of the table, which the widow had cleared and laid for coffee.

Anyone unacquainted with Reverend Nordström would never have guessed that this islander was a man of the cloth. Thirty years of ministering to souls in the islands had wrought changes on the refined curate who had come out here after his ordination in Uppsala. A miserable stipend had forced him to scratch a living from his glebe and from the sea. When these failed to produce sufficient, he had to appeal to the goodwill of his parishioners and, in order to encourage that goodwill, he had adapted his social manner to the environment in which he lived. The islanders' benificence, however, tended to take the form of coffee with schnapps or other kinds of hospitality that had to be consumed on the spot and thus did nothing to enhance the prosperity of the manse – indeed, they tended rather to have a deleterious effect on the physical and moral condition of the recipient. In any case, the islanders felt they got little or no reward for the small wooden chapel they had built. Their own harsh experience had taught them that God helps those who help themselves 'when in peril on the sea', and they seemed constitutionally incapable of recognising any connection between a sudden easterly gale and the Augsburg Confession. The result was that their church attendance, which was discouraged anyway by the distance they had to row, if not rendered impossible by adverse winds, had become more of a local market for them to meet their acquaintances, do business and listen to any announcements. The minister, in fact, was the only local dignitary the islanders came in contact with since the county constable lived far away on the mainland and was never called upon to deal with legal disputes anyway: these tended to be settled man to man either by means of some head-butting or by getting together over half a jug of schnapps.

As already mentioned, the minister had set off for the town with his fish-cage to sell the fish he had taken from the sea himself and after running into the storm he had been driven before the wind. With his gun well stowed in its leather case, his provisions and book in a sealskin bag, wet and chilled to the bone, he had reached light and warmth and, after rubbing his eyes, been given a seat at the table and offered coffee. Not a trace of Latin and Greek was evident any longer in the figure sitting there in the light of the fire and two candles: he was now a cross between farmer and seaman. His hands, which had once been white and done nothing but turn the pages of books, were now brown and rough as bark, with liver marks caused by sun and salt water, hard and calloused from rowing, hauling the sheets and holding the tiller. His nails were bitten down and black-edged from contact with the soil and tools; his ears sprouted a matted tangle of hair and were pierced to take leaden rings as curatives for flux and discharges; a clock-key made of some sort of yellow metal with a cornelian in it was attached by a braid of hair to the leather pocket stitched on to his woollen jersey; his wet woollen stockings had holes over his big toes and the twisting movements of his feet under the table appeared to be an attempt to conceal them; his jersey was yellowy brown under the arms from sweat, and the fly of his trousers gaped half open for lack of sufficient buttons.

He took a briar pipe from his trouser pocket and everyone maintained a respectful silence as he tapped it against the edge of the table so that a little molehill of ashes and dottle dropped on the floor. His hand was unsteady and the filling of the pipe was not straightforward – in fact, the process was far too long-winded not to cause disquiet.

'And how are you this evening, minister? Not too well, it seems,' the widow said while the pipe was being filled.

The minister raised his drooping head and peered around and up at the beams, as if looking for whoever was speaking.

'What, me?' he said, pressing a pinch of tobacco on the outside of the bowl of the pipe. Then he shook his head as if wanting to be left in peace and sank back into vague and melancholy thoughts.

Carlsson, who perceived the state he was in, whispered to

the widow:

'He's not sober.' And thinking he should intervene he took the coffee pot and filled the minister's cup. He placed the schnapps bottle alongside and, with a slight bow, invited him to help himself.

The old man lifted his grey head and gave Carlsson a crushing look, as if trying to frighten him out of his wits. Pushing the cup away in disgust, he spat out:

'Got your feet under the table here, have you, fellow?' And then he turned to the widow and said:

'Give me a cup of coffee, Madame Flod!'

Then he sank back into deep silence for a while, possibly contemplating the good old times and the growing impudence of the common people these days.

'Bloody farm-hand!' he said with another snort. 'Get out there and give Robert a hand!'

Before disappearing out through the door Carlsson made an attempt at flattery but was immediately cut short with a 'Don't get above yourself, you!'

The minister fortified himself with a swig from the cup.

'Have you got your nets out?' he snapped at the widow, who was trying to cobble together some excuse for her farm-hand.

'Oh yes, God help us, the whole lot of them! Who'd have believed at six o'clock that it would turn into a storm by nightfall. And I know Gusten – he'd rather go to the bottom himself than leave the nets in the shallows overnight.' The old woman was about to open the waterworks.

'Nonsense! He'll manage them all right!' the minister comforted her.

'Oh, don't say that, Reverend! It's not the nets that matter, though they don't come cheap – just so long as the boy doesn't come to any harm ...'

'He surely wouldn't be so stupid as to go and pull them up in this weather, with the sea running as it is?'

'That's just the sort of thing you can expect him to do. He takes after his father in being very careful with what he owns and he'd be quite capable of risking his life rather than lose the nets.'

'Well, Madame Flod, if that's the way he's inclined then the devil himself can't help him! The fishing's good, mind you. We were out by the Alkobbarne rocks the other day and caught a hundred and twenty dozen in six casts.'

'My oh my! And were they fat?'

'Indeed they were. Fat as butter! Now then, Madame Flod, tell me what's all this I'm hearing about you thinking of going and getting married? Any truth in it?'

'Lord above!' the widow exclaimed. 'Is that what people are saying? It's just dreadful the way people go round gossiping and saying things.'

'Not that it's any concern of mine,' the minister continued, 'but if what people are saying is true and you've got the farmhand in mind, it would be a pity for your lad.'

'There'd be no risk in it for Gusten – and many people have had worse stepfathers.'

'I see. I can see the way things are going anyway. Is your old body so aflame that you can't hold out any longer? Well, well, it's the way of all flesh, I suppose – ho, ho, ho, ho!'

'Wouldn't you like a drop of schnapps in your coffee, Reverend?' the old woman interrupted, growing worried at the indelicate turn the conversation was taking.

'Thank you, Madame Flod, that's kind of you. I'll take it straight this time, perhaps. And I should be off to bed, though I don't think you've had one made up for me yet.'

She decided that Carlsson and Robert could sleep in the kitchen and so Lotten was sent off to make up a bed for the minister in Carlsson's attic.

The minister gave an enormous yawn, scratched one foot against the other, stroked his forehead and bald pate with his hand as if trying to wipe away nameless worries and, bit by bit, in a series of small nods, his head sank down to the table-top, where it came to rest supported on his chin.

Realising the way things were going, the widow went over to him, carefully put her hand on his shoulder, patted him gently and asked in a supplicant tone:

'Minister dear, won't you read us a few words of comfort before we go to bed? Think of me, an old woman whose son is out in peril on the sea.'

'A short passage, right, right! Pass me the book then – it's in my bag over there.'

The widow fetched his leather bag and took out a black book adorned with a gold cross, which the minister liked to produce as a sort of travelling medicine case in order to offer fortifying tonics to old women and to the sick. Solemnly, as if a piece of the church had entered her humble cottage, she carefully carried the book of mysteries in both hands like a hot, fresh loaf, gently pushed the cup away from the minister, dried a place on the table with her apron and laid the holy book down in front of his heavy head.

'Minister dear,' the widow whispered as the wind roared in the chimney, 'here is the book.'

'Good, good,' the minister answered as if asleep, then stretched out his arm without raising his head, groped round for the coffee cup and nudged its handle with his fingers, knocking over the cup so that two streams of schnapps ran across the greasy table.

'Oh dear, oh dear, oh dear!' the widow moaned, managing to rescue the book. 'This is not going to work. You're sleepy and need your bed.'

The minister, however, was already snoring, his arms resting on the table and his middle finger sticking out in a silly gesture as if pointing towards some invisible and, for the moment, unattainable goal.

'How in Heaven's name are we going to get him to bed?' the widow wailed at the girls, utterly at a loss as to how to stir the sleeping man whom she knew to have a vile temper if woken up after he had been drinking. He could not be left in the kitchen because the girls slept there, nor could he be put in the parlour because that might lead to gossip. The three women circled the minister like mice trying to bell a cat, but none of them dared try.

In the meantime, however, the fire had gone out, the wind

was finding ways in through the window-panes and draughty walls and the old minister, who was sitting there in stockinged soles, must have begun to feel the cold because all of a sudden his head came up, his mouth gaped opened wide and he uttered three screams – just like a fox in its death throes – that made the women jump.

'I think I must have sneezed,' the minister said, rising from the table and walking with his eyes shut to the window bench, where he sat down, stretched out on his back and fell asleep with a long sigh and his hands crossed over his chest.

There was no hope of moving him now and neither Carlsson nor Robert, who had come back in, was prepared to risk touching him.

'Watch yourselves – he'll fight you!' Robert informed them. 'Just give him a pillow and throw a blanket over him and he'll sleep until morning.'

The widow took the girls into the parlour with her, Robert would sleep in the loft over the storeroom and Carlsson could go to his attic. The lights were put out and the kitchen fell silent.

Soon the whole house was asleep, more or less peacefully.

At cockcrow the following morning when Madame Flod rose to wake them, the minister and Robert were already away. The storm had eased a little and cold white autumn clouds were sailing in from the east towards the mainland in a sky that was fresh and blue. Around eight o'clock the widow set off down to the eastern headland to see whether there was any sign of Gusten's boat out in the bay. Now and then a reefed square-rigged sail would appear in the channel between the islands, disappear and then reappear. The sea, blue as steel, was still running high and the outermost skerries hovered like mirages, hanging there on airy veils as if they had floated up from the water and were about to disperse into the ether like night mists. Young mergansers were swimming in the bays and round the headlands, skittering over the waves when they saw a sea-eagle flying ponderously in their direction, diving and coming up again, and then skittering once more so that the water splashed up in front of them. Whenever the widow heard the screeching of gulls and saw them fly up from the rocks out there, she knew a sail would appear – and appear it did, only to steer clear of the island and bear away north or south.

There was a cold wind and the white clouds and the wind hurt her eyes. Tired of waiting, she went back into the wood and began picking cowberries in her apron since she had to be doing something to keep her anxiety at bay. Her son was, after all, the most precious thing she had; she had not felt half so worried that evening when she had stood by the stile and watched another vague hope disappear into the darkness. But her boy was even more precious to her now, perhaps because she had begun to feel that he would soon be leaving her. The gossip and the minister's words the night before had lighted a touch-paper and there was soon going to be a bang. Whose eyebrows it would singe was yet to be decided, but it was clear enough that it was bound to singe someone.

So she slowly trotted off homewards and arrived at the cluster of oak trees. A hum of voices was coming from down by the jetty, and through the oak leaves she could see people moving round the boathouse, all of them talking at the same time, discussing, explaining and bickering. Something had happened while she was away, but what?

With her curiosity whipped up by anxiety, she braced her legs and went down the slope to find out what was happening. When she reached the fence she could see the stern of the herring-boat: they were home safely, then, and must have rowed all the way round the other side of the island.

Norman's voice was clearly audible as he recounted the course of events:

'He went to the bottom like a stone before coming up again. But then death struck him straight in the left eye – it was just like putting out a light.'

'Oh, Lord Jesus, is he dead?' the widow screamed and rushed over the fence, but no one heard her because Rundqvist, down in the boat, was continuing the necrologue:

'Then we got the grapnel in him and when the fluke stuck

77

in his back ...'

The old woman was behind the drying-frames where the nets were hanging and she could not get through but, through the nets, as though in a mirror draped with mourning crêpe, she could see all the people of the farm leaning, hanging and crawling round a greyish body stowed in the boat. She began to scream and tried to get under the nets but the birch-bark floats caught in her hair and the sinker-leads whipped her like a scourge.

'What in the name of Jesus have we caught in the flounder net?' Rundqvist yelled, seeing there was something alive in the mesh. 'Oh no, I do believe it's the mistress!'

'Is he dead?' Madame Flod shouted as loudly as she could. 'Is he dead?'

'Dead as a dead dog!'

The widow freed herself and ran to the jetty. There she saw Gusten, bare-headed and bent over in the bottom of the boat – but he was moving, and under him there was a large hairy body.

'Is that you, mother?' Gusten greeted her without turning round. 'See the whopper we've caught.'

The widow's eyes widened at the sight of the fat grey seal Gusten was in the process of skinning. She knew that a seal was not an everyday event and the meat could be eaten – such as it was – and the oil would be sufficient to treat numerous pairs of boots, and the skin would presumably be worth twenty kronor or so. But herring for the winter was much more urgent and she could not see a single fin in the boat. Forgetting both the return of the prodigal son and the unexpected seal, her mood turned to one of dejection and reproach:

'And what about the herring, then?'

'It wasn't so easy to get at the herring,' Gusten answered, 'and anyway we can always buy some, but you don't get a grey seal every day of the week.'

'That's what you always say, Gusten, but it's a downright disgrace to be away for three days and not bring any fish home. What are we supposed to eat through the winter, do you think?'

She failed to win any support, however, because they were all sick of herring and meat was meat when all was said and done; and so the hunters with their wonderful stories of their adventure held everyone's attention.

'Ah well,' Carlsson said, never one to miss the opportunity to score points, 'if we didn't have the land, we would run right out of food.'

No seine-netting was done that day because the big washing boiler had to be put on to boil the oil, and the kitchen was full of roasting and boiling and everyone drank their coffee with dashes of schnapps. The sealskin was stretched up on the south wall of the barn as a trophy to be shown off to the accompaniment of endless post-mortems; every passing sceptic had to stick his fingers in the pellet holes and hear how the shot had gone in, where the seal had crawled up on a rock, what Gusten had said to Norman just as he was about to fire the shot, and how the dead seal had behaved in its final moment when 'its life was cut off like cutting a thread'.

Carlsson had no choice but to take a back seat during those days but he was secretly whetting his steel, and when the seine-netting was finally over, he took the rudder of the boat and sailed into town with Norman and Lotten.

*

When Madame Flod came down to the jetty to welcome them on their return from the town Carlsson was all meekness and solicitude and the widow realised straightaway that something had happened while they had been away.

After supper she invited him into the parlour for him to account for and hand over the money, after which she asked him to take a seat and tell her about the trip. This proved to be heavy going since Carlsson did not seem at all keen to reveal much, but the widow had no intention of letting him go before getting the story out of him.

'Well, Carlsson,' she said, trying to milk him for information, 'I suppose you went to the professor's place?'

'I popped in for a while, of course,' Carlsson answered, obviously discomfited by the memory.

'And how were they?'

'They sent their regards to everyone on the farm and were kind enough to invite me to breakfast. Their flat is unbelievably posh and we got on fine.'

'Well, well, and the food was good, was it?'

'Yes, we had lobster and mushrooms and a glass of porter as well.'

'You'll have seen the girls, I suppose?'

'Yes, of course,' Carlsson answered frankly.

'And they were the same as ever, I imagine?'

They most certainly were not but, knowing how much it would have pleased the widow to hear it, Carlsson did not answer her question.

'They were all very pleasant and we went to Berns' Restaurant in the evening to listen to music. And I treated them to sherry-cobbler and sandwiches. It was all really nice, I can tell you.'

That is not, in reality, how things had happened at all, and it had been anything but pleasant. What actually happened was that Ida was away and Carlsson had been received in the kitchen by Lina, who gave him a half of beer at the kitchen table. Then the professor's wife had come in, said hello, told Lina to have a lobster delivered since they were expecting a guest that evening, and then she had left. When the two of them were left on their own Lina had initially been rather stiff, but Carlsson plugged away and managed to extract from her that Ida had received his letter and read it out aloud in the kitchen one evening while her fiancé was there drinking porter and Lina was cleaning mushrooms. They had nearly died laughing at it, especially when the fiancé put on a clergyman's voice and read the letter aloud twice. Funniest of all had been the bits about 'old Carlsson' and 'his final moments', and when they reached the part about 'temptations and straying from the straight and narrow' the fiancé – who was a drayman – suggested they go out and sample the temptations at Berns's, which they duly did, and he treated them to sherry-cobbler and sandwiches.

Whether Lina's story had rattled Carlsson so much that his recollections had become confused, or whether his desire to be in the drayman's shoes was so intense that he simply assumed the latter's enviable role as host, swapping places with the lobster-eating stranger, drinking the fiancé's porter and eating Lina's mushrooms – whatever the reason may have been, that is the picture he painted for the widow. And it had the desired effect, which was the main thing. Once the story was told, he felt calmer and ready to make his move. The boys were out at sea, Rundqvist had gone to bed, and the girls had finished for the day.

'What's all this talk I hear round the parish – it keeps coming up all the time?' he began.

'What are they all on about now?' the widow asked.

'Oh, just the same old stuff – that we're thinking of getting married.'

'Pooh – we've been hearing that for ages.'

'I know, but it's not right that people should go round saying things that aren't true. I really can't understand that kind of behaviour,' Carlsson said slyly.

'Yes, and what would a spry young fellow like you be doing with an old woman like me?'

'Oh, age is no problem as far as I'm concerned. If I were to think of getting married it wouldn't be to some hussy that can't do anything and doesn't know anything. Lust is one thing, marriage another, isn't that right? Lust – earthly lust – passes like a puff of smoke and all these promises to be faithful are worth about as much as a pinch of snuff as soon as someone else comes along and offers you a cigar. But me, missus, I'm the kind that would keep my promise if I got married – that's how I've always been and anyone who says any different is a liar.'

The widow pricked up her ears at this and began to scent something in the air.

'So what about Ida, then? I thought there was something serious between you and her, Carlsson?' said Madame Flod, testing the waters.

'Oh, nothing wrong with Ida in her own way and I'd only

have to wag my finger and she'd come like a shot. But she hasn't got the right turn of mind for me – she's worldly and vain and I think she'd prefer to stray off the straight and narrow. And anyway, I have to admit I'm getting on a bit myself and I'm past all that silliness. I'll tell you straight, if I *were* thinking of getting married I'd go for someone older and sensible, someone with the right turn of mind. I don't rightly know how to put it but I think you understand what I'm getting at because you're a sensible woman yourself, you are indeed.'

The widow had sat down at the table in order to follow Carlsson's hummings and hawings, this way and that way, and to be ready to say her Amen the moment he finally got round to his Yes.

'Ah well, Carlsson,' she said pulling a different strand out of the tangled skein, 'you must surely have thought of the widow over at Åvassa, sitting there all alone and wanting nothing better than to get married again?'

'Her? No...o! Oh, I know her all right but she hasn't got the right turn of mind and that's what matters to me. Money and fancy clothes and putting on airs – those things don't count with me. I'm not like that, and anybody who really knows me will tell you that.'

They seemed to have nibbled round all the edges of the topic and one of them would have to have the last word while there was still a chance to do so.

'So, had you thought of anyone in particular then, Carlsson?' It was the widow who risked taking the bold step.

'Thought of and thought of! I haven't really thought of anything at all yet, but a fellow gets to thinking of this and thinking of that and once he's thought he speaks. I keep my mouth shut, I do, so that no one can come along later and say I've been trying to lead anyone on – that's not the sort of fellow I am.'

By this point the old woman was not quite sure which direction things were going but felt she should continue testing the water.

'Well, my dear Carlsson, if you've still got Ida in mind you can't really go and seriously think about anyone else.'

'Ida? Hm, that foxy so-and-so! I wouldn't have her if you threw her at me! No, she'll have to be better than that. Someone who at least owns the clothes on her own back, and it wouldn't go amiss if she had a bit more, too – not that I'm looking for it, mind you, I'm not that sort.'

They had now gone round in so many circles that the whole business was in danger of stalling unless the widow gave it a further nudge.

'Now then, Carlsson, what would you say to you and me giving it a try together?'

Carlsson threw up his hands as if wanting to rebuff at once any suspicion that he had been harbouring such a shameful thought.

'Oh no, surely that's out of the question!' he protested. 'We shouldn't talk about it, not even think about it! I know what they'd all be saying – he just took her for her money. But that's not my way, that's not what I'm like. No, we shouldn't even mention the idea again, not ever. Promise me now, and shake my hand on it (he held out his hand at this point) that we'll never ever mention this again. Here, shake on it!'

But the widow did not want to shake his hand on it, she wanted to talk it through from beginning to end.

'Why shouldn't we talk about something that might well be worth doing? You know I'm getting on a bit, Carlsson, but Gusten is not yet man enough to take on the farm. I need someone at my side, someone to help me out, but I do understand that you don't want to work for nothing and wear yourself out for others – so the only way out is for us to get married. Let people talk, they'll chatter anyway, and if you don't have anything special against me I can see nothing to stop us. Tell me, do you have anything against me?'

'I've got nothing against you at all, nothing – but what about all the blessed gossip there'll be? And I don't see Gusten being too pleased about us being together.'

'Rubbish! If you're not up to dealing with him I certainly am. I may be getting on in years but I'm not that old, and I'll tell you this, Carlsson, just between you and me ... you'll find me as good as any of these young lassies when it comes to the other business ...'

The ice was broken and a flood of plans and proposals followed: how to tell Gusten, how to arrange the wedding and so on. And the discussions lasted a long time, so long that the widow had to put on the coffee pot and get out the schnapps bottle. In fact, they lasted far into the night, and a little beyond.

CHAPTER V

There is trouble at the third reading of the banns. They go to
communion and celebrate their wedding but still do not get into
the bridal bed.

It is a fact that no man receives more praise than when he dies
or less praise than when he marries, as Carlsson was soon to
discover. Gusten had roared like a hungry grey seal, arguing and
raging for three days, during which Carlsson took himself off on
a short trip on the pretext of business. Old Flod was disinterred
from his resting place, turned inside out and found to have
been one of the paragons of humankind, whereas Carlsson
was inspected like a suit of old clothes and found to have a
stained lining. They discovered he had been both a navvy and
a hawker of Bibles, thrown out of three jobs and walked out of
at least one, and – according to an unsubstantiated rumour –
had been up before the bench for brawling. All this was thrown
in Madame Flod's face but her fire was now kindled and, with
the prospect of the end of widowhood, she seemed to perk up,
to come alive and develop a will of her own, and so she took
everything that was thrown at her.

Most of the hostility towards Carlsson arose from him being
an outsider who, by deed of marriage, was about to acquire
land and water that the locals had come to think of as being,
at least to some extent, common property. Since the farm
had been settled on Madame Flod as a jointure and since she
probably still had many years to live, her son's prospects of
coming into his own had diminished. Henceforth his position
on the farm would be little different from that of a farm-hand
and, moreover, he would be subject to the authority and

good will of the former farm-hand, who also happened to be a recent incomer. Little wonder, then, that this demotion enraged Gusten to the extent that he had angry words with his mother, threatening to go to court and sue in order to get his future stepfather shown the door. And when Carlsson arrived home from his little trip wearing the late lamented Flod's black Sunday coat and sealskin cap – which he had received as morning gifts after that first amorous encounter – Gusten's mood was at its worst. He said nothing but he bribed Rundqvist to play a trick, and one morning when they all came to breakfast there was a cloth covering a pile of invisible objects in front of Carlsson's chair. Carlsson, not suspecting any mischief, picked up the cloth and found his end of the table covered with all the rubbish he had collected in his sack and forgotten about after hiding it under his bed up in the attic. There were empty lobster and sardine tins, mushroom jars, a porter bottle, an endless array of corks, a cracked flower-pot and a great deal more of the same.

Carlsson's eyes flashed but he had no idea on whom to vent his spleen. Rundqvist provided a lightning conductor by explaining that this sort of 'teasing' was common in the islands when someone was about to get married. Unfortunately, however, Gusten entered just then and expressed his surprise that the rag and bone man had come so early in the autumn since he did not usually turn up until after the New Year. At which Norman seized the moment to inform everyone that the rag and bone man was not coming early and that these things were Carlsson's souvenirs of Ida: Rundqvist had merely wanted to play a practical joke on him now that everything was over between the two of them.

A sharp exchange of words followed with the result that Gusten went to the manse and managed to have Carlsson's wedding delayed by six months because of some doubt about his official papers. Carlsson did what he could to erase this black mark from his book by using any and every opportunity open to him. Initially he had taken on his new role with some degree of solemnity but, when this failed to work, he decided to try a more humorous approach, at least with the people on the farm. That worked well except with Gusten, who continued to wage vicious submarine warfare with no sign of any desire for reconciliation.

Winter passed in its usual quiet way with timber-cutting, net-making and ice-fishing, relieved by the occasional game of cards, coffee and schnapps sessions, a Christmas feast and shooting longtailed ducks. And then it was spring again. The flights of eider duck tempted people out onto the water, but Carlsson put all their efforts into the spring working of the land in order to guarantee the bumper harvest necessary to make up for the expense of the wedding, especially since the intention was to put on the kind of magnificent celebration that would be remembered for years to come.

And with the migratory birds came the summer guests, the professor nodding his approval and saying everything was 'wunderbar' just as he had the year before, but even more so now that there was going to be a wedding. Ida, fortunately, was not with them: she had left their service in April and seemed likely to be getting married herself soon. Her successor was not particularly prepossessing and Carlsson, anyway, had too many irons in the fire to want to get involved – he had all the cards in his hand and had no intention of losing the game.

The banns were read on Midsummer's Day and the wedding itself was to be held between haymaking and harvesting, when there was always a short period of calm in their work, both on the farm and at sea.

An unpleasant change in Carlsson's demeanour became apparent after the banns were published and Madame Flod was the first to experience it. In accordance with local custom they had, of course, been living as man and wife ever since their engagement and Carlsson, who still had the postponement hanging over his head, had taken care to trim his sails to suit the prevailing wind but, once the danger was over, he stuck his nose in the air and showed his claws. Since Madame Flod thought she had a firm grip on things, this had no effect on her other than to make her show her teeth – or as many of them as she had left – and the clash came at the third reading of the banns.

Apart from Lotten, everyone on the island had made the journey to church for the communion service. They had, as usual, taken the smallest boat possible in order to cut the amount of work needed should they be forced to row, and so the boat was crowded, all the more so since they had lunch baskets with them, as well as ten pounds of orfe for the minister, a couple of pounds of candles for the parish clerk and numerous changes of clothing – not to mention sails and oars, bailers and buckets, stools and foot-rests.

As was the custom they had eaten a lavish breakfast and jugs and half-bottles had been passed round among them during the morning. It was also hot out on the water and none of them wanted to row, which led to some quarrelling among the men, none of whom had any desire to arrive at the church in a sweaty state. The women had calmed things down and by the time they sailed into the bay where the church was and heard the bells they had not heard for so long the quarrel had been set aside. As it was only the first ringing of the bells they had time to spare and Madame Flod went up to the manse with the orfe. The minister was still shaving and not in the best of tempers.

'Rare visitors to the church today – we don't often see the people from Hemsö!' he greeted her, wiping his razor with his forefinger.

Carlsson, who was carrying the fish, was nevertheless allowed into the kitchen to have a dram.

Then they took the candles to the parish clerk and were given another dram there.

Everyone finally gathered on the slope outside the church, inspected the horses of the big farmers, read the memorial inscriptions and greeted acquaintances. Carlsson took himself off to one side while Madame Flod paid a short visit to Old Man Flod's grave and then, when the bells chimed and rattled in the belfry, the congregation went quietly in. Since the old church burned down the people of Hemsö had not had a pew of their own and were forced to stand in the aisle. It was dreadfully hot and, standing there in that large space and feeling like strangers, they started sweating with sheer embarrassment since they looked like a row of sinners lined up ready for the stool of penitence. It was eleven o'clock before they even reached the sermon hymn and by that time the Hemsö folk had already crossed and uncrossed their legs and shifted from foot to foot a couple of dozen times. The blazing sun shone in and beads of sweat formed on their foreheads, but they were trapped as if in a vice and had no chance of moving into the shade. Then the churchwarden stepped forward and put up Hymn No. 158, the organ piped the prelude and the sexton took up the first verse. They all joined in heartily since they were expecting the sermon immediately afterwards – but then came verse two and verse three.

'They can't really be intending to go through all eighteen, can they?' Rundqvist whispered to Norman.

But they could. Meanwhile, in the doorway to the vestry, Reverend Nordström's angry face could be seen looking out over his congregation defiantly and challengingly, determined to give them a severe dressing-down now that he at last had them in his clutches.

So they sang their way through all eighteen verses and it was half past eleven before the minister finally went up into the pulpit. By then they were limp, so limp that their heads slumped on their chests and they fell asleep. But their slumbers were short-lived for the minister instantly yelled at them so that the sleepers jumped, jerked back their heads and stared like idiots at their neighbours as if asking whether the church was on fire.

Carlsson and Madame Flod had pushed their way so far forward that it was impossible for them to retreat to the door without causing a scandal. The widow was weeping with sheer exhaustion and because her boots were so tight that they were pinching her feet more and more as the heat rose. She turned now and then and gave her fiancé a beseeching look as if imploring him to carry her down to the sea but, standing there in old Flod's roomy horse-leather boots, he was so taken up by the service that his only response to the impatient woman was to treat her to a rancorous glare. The rest of their company, however, had managed to ease their way aft and into the shade of the organ loft where it was cool. Gusten had found a fire extinguisher there, on which he sat down and took Clara on his knee.

Rundqvist, with Norman beside him, was leaning on a pillar when the sermon began. The minister went in for plain speaking and the sermon lasted an hour and a half. He took as his text the parable of the wise and foolish virgins and since none of the men felt it applied to them most of them fell asleep, sitting, hanging or standing.

After the passage of half an hour Norman prodded Rundqvist, who was leaning forward head in hand as if he was feeling sick, and pointed his thumb at Clara and Gusten over on the fire extinguisher. Rundqvist turned round carefully and his eyes widened as if he was seeing the devil himself, then he shook his head and gave a knowing grin: Clara was sitting with her tongue hanging out and her eyes shut as if she was asleep and having bad dreams, whereas Gusten was staring fixedly at the minister as if swallowing his every word and straining to hear the sand run through the hour-glass.

'Aren't they just awful!' Rundqvist whispered, taking slow, cautious steps backwards and putting his heels down carefully so as not to make too much noise on the tiles. Norman had already read what was in Rundqvist's mind and, slippery as an eel, he slid out into the churchyard, soon followed by Rundqvist. Then the two deserters made their way down to the boat.

There was a cool sea-breeze outside and that, together with the hasty refreshments they partook of, soon revived them. As silently as they had left, they returned to the church and looked at Clara and Gusten, who were both asleep; his arms had moved up from her waist, high enough for Rundqvist to consider it only proper to move them down a little, at which Gusten woke and took a new hold on his prey, as if someone had been trying to take the girl away from him.

The sermon lasted for another half an hour and then a half-hour of hymn singing followed before communion started. The sacraments were received with profound emotion and Rundqvist wept, but after receiving the sacraments at the altar Madame Flod tried to force her way into a seat in a pew, which almost caused a row before she was turned away. She spent the last half-hour outside the churchwarden's pew, standing on her heels as if the tiles were too hot for the soles of her feet, and when the minister finally read out the banns she became furious because people started looking at her.

At last it was all over and they rushed down to the boats. Madame Flod could bear it no longer and as soon as she had received everyone's congratulations in the churchyard she took off her boots and carried them down to the boat, where she stuck her feet in the water and picked a quarrel with Carlsson. Then they all pounced on the lunch-bags and there was a great shindig when it was discovered that the pancakes were gone. Rundqvist thought they had possibly been forgotten whereas Norman suggested that someone must have eaten them on the way over – maliciously throwing suspicion Carlsson's way.

Once they were in the boat Carlsson remembered he had a barrel of tar to collect from the church shed. That led to an uproar, with the women all yelling that they were not having tar in the boat, not on your life, not when they had their new dresses on. Carlsson fetched the barrel anyway and stowed it aboard, which led to a row about who was going to sit close to the dangerous object.

'What am I to sit on, then?' Madame Flod whined.

'Pull up your skirts and sit on your backside,' Carlsson answered, much more sure of himself now the banns had been read.

'What was that you said?' the widow snarled.

'I said what I said! Now sit in the boat and let's get going.'

'And who gives the orders at sea, if I may ask?' Gusten interrupted, feeling that his position was being threatened.

Then he sat at the helm, had the sail hoisted and took hold of the sheet. The boat was so laden it lay deep in the water, the wind was very weak, the sun was scorching hot and tempers were frayed. The boat moved forward 'like a louse across a tarred plank' and a dram for the menfolk did little to help. Patience was soon exhausted and the silence that had ruled for a little while was broken by Carlsson who wanted them to take down the sail and row. But Gusten was against it: 'Wait a bit – once we're outside the skerries we'll sail all right'.

They waited. A dark blue streak appeared out in the sound between the islands and they could hear the noise of the waves against the outer skerries. A strong easterly wind was rising and the sails began to fill. As they passed round a headland the wind caught them and the boat heeled over, rose and shot forward with her wake swirling astern. Everyone had another dram at this, the mood becoming lighter as they made good speed. But the wind was freshening and the lee gunwale of the boat dipped below the water but ran on driven briskly from abaft the beam. Carlsson became afraid, clung on to the thwart and demanded they should bear up and reef the sail.

Gusten did not answer, instead he hauled on the sheet so that water came in.

Carlsson leapt up in a wild fury and wanted to put out an oar, but the old woman grabbed his coat and pulled him down again.

'Sit down in the boat, for Jesus' sake, man!' she roared.

Carlsson sat down, white in the face, but he did not stay sitting for long before jumping up again with his coat tails flying. He was frantic.

'Merciful God, that bugger's sprung a leak now,' he yelled, flapping his coat tails.

'Who's leaking?' they all asked in chorus.

'The barrel, the bloody barrel!'

'Oh, Lord Jesus!' they chorused now, all moving to make room for the flood of tar that was gliding this way and that with the movements of the boat.

'Sit down in the boat,' Gusten raged, 'or I'll have you all in the water!'

Carlsson got up again just as a gust was about to hit them.

Rundqvist saw the danger in time, carefully got off his hind-quarters and gave him such a clout that it felled him. A fight seemed inevitable but Madame Flod, by now quite beside herself, decided to intervene.

She grabbed her intended by the collar of his coat and gave him a shaking.

'What kind of pathetic creature are you? Have you never been out at sea before? For goodness' sake behave like a man and sit down in the boat!'

Carlsson became angry and tore himself free, losing a piece of his coat collar in the process.

'So now you're going to rip up my clothes, are you, you old bag!' he shrieked, putting his boots up on the gunwales to protect them from the tar.

'What do you think you're talking about?' the widow fired back. 'Your coat? Who did you get the coat from, then? How dare you call me an old bag – small fry like you with nothing to offer...'

'Shut up!' Carlsson, roared, struck to the quick on the most delicate point of all. 'Shut up – or I'll give you some real home truths!'

Gusten, thinking that things were starting to get out of hand, began yodelling a schottische and Norman and Rundqvist joined in. The poisonous conversation died down and they all turned instead on their common enemy, Reverend Nordström, who had had them standing there for five hours and singing eighteen verses. The bottle was passed round again, the wind eased off, tempers calmed down and finally, to everyone's relief, the boat slid into the bay and bumped into the jetty.

And now the preparations for the wedding – which was to last for three days – got underway. They slaughtered a pig and a cow, bought fifty gallons of schnapps, preserved herring in salt and bay leaves, baked, scrubbed, brewed, boiled, fried, and ground coffee beans. Gusten went round looking mysterious while all this was going on – he let others make all the decisions and offered no opinions of his own. Carlsson, however, spent most of his time sitting at the bureau writing and doing accounts – he also made trips to Dalarö and organised everything that was to happen.

The day before the wedding Gusten packed his bag early in the morning, took his gun and went out. His mother woke and asked where he was off to. Gusten replied that he intended to go and see whether the orfe had come up, and off he went.

He had provisioned his boat with food for several days and also included bedding, a coffee pot and the other items necessary for a stay out in the skerries. He set sail at once and instead of putting into the bays to see if the orfe had come into the warm, sandy, shallow waters to 'bathe', as the islanders call it, he set a straight course out between the islands.

They were coming to the end of July and it was a beautifully clear morning with a sky as blue-white as skimmed milk and with the islands, holms, skerries and rocks lying so softly on the water that it was impossible to say whether they were part of the earth or part of the heavens. On the islands nearest land spruce and alder were growing and goosanders, scoters, mergansers and gulls floated on the water between the headlands; on the farther islands there were only dwarf pines, and guillemots and black parrot-like razorbills clustered boldly round the boat in an effort to lead the hunter away from their nests hidden in rocky crevices. Then the skerries became lower and barer and the only trees to be seen were the occasional rowan, with a cloud of mosquitoes swaying in the breeze above it, or a pine, left there to support the nesting-boxes from which the islanders would gather their share of eider and merganser eggs. Out beyond that lay the open sea, where the pirate skua squabbled with terns and herring gulls and where the sea-eagle flew on slow and heavy wing-beats to swoop on any drifting eider in its path. Gusten, half-lying at the rudder with his pipe in his mouth, steered a course out to the most distant skerry, letting himself be carried along on a warm southerly breeze, and by nine o'clock he was stepping ashore on Norsten. It was a tiny rocky island, just a couple of acres with a small hollow in the middle. Only one or two sparse rowan trees grew among the rocks but spindle, that lovely bush with its fire-red berries, filled the crevices, while the hollow was covered with a deep carpet of heather, crowberry and cloudberries that were beginning to turn yellow and ripen. Here and there juniper bushes spread out as if they had been trampled flat on the rocky slabs and seemed to be clinging on by their nails in order not to be blown away. Gusten felt thoroughly at home here, knew every stone, knew where to lift a juniper bush and find a sitting eider duck that would peck his trouser leg but let him stroke her back. He poked his forked stick into a crack in the rocks, pulled out some razorbills and wrung their necks to have them for breakfast. The Hemsö islanders had their herring grounds out here and, together with another fishing crew, they had built a hut to provide them with shelter at night. Gusten made his way there, found the key in its usual place under the eaves and carried in his things. The hut consisted of a single windowless room with bunks, one above the other like shelves, a stove, a three-legged stool and a table.

When he had stowed away his things he climbed up on the roof, opened the chimney hatch and climbed down again. Taking the matches from their place under a beam, he lit the stove, in which the last visitor had remembered – as was customary – to put a bundle of dry firewood ready for those who came next. Then he put on a pan of potatoes, placed a layer of salted fish over them and smoked his pipe while he waited.

Once he had eaten and had a dram he took his gun and went down to the boat, where he had left the decoys. He rowed out and anchored the decoys off a headland, then crept into a hide built of stones and brushwood. The decoys lay there rising and falling on the long, slow swell but failed to attract any eider. The wait was a long one and, growing tired of it, he began wandering round the rocks on the shore looking for an otter but coming across nothing but a couple of black adders and the odd wasps' nest in among the bright purple loosestrife and dry lyme-grass.

He did not seem too worried about catching anything anyway and was wandering for the sake of wandering, to avoid being at home or simply because he liked being out here where no one could see him and no one hear him.

After dinner he lay down in the hut for a sleep and at suppertime rowed out with his cod line to try his luck with that. The sea was now dead calm and he could see the land lying stretched out like a thin ribbon of smoke in the golden path of the setting sun. Everything round him was as silent as a windless night so he could hear the thud of rowlocks three miles away. Meanwhile, seals swam round at a respectful distance, poking up their plump heads, barking, blowing and diving again.

The fish were really taking and he hauled in several white-bellied cod, which gasped for water with their large but harmless mouths and scowled at the sun as they were pulled up from the darkness of the deep and swung in over the rail.

He had kept to the north side of the skerry so it was not until evening suddenly came on and it was time for him to go ashore that he noticed smoke rising from the chimney of the hut. Wondering what was happening, he made his way quickly to the cottage.

'Is that you?' came a voice which he recognised as that of the minister.

'Well, I'll be ... so it's you, Reverend!' Gusten said in amazement on seeing the minister sitting by the glowing stove frying herring. 'Have you come out on your own?'

'Yes, I came out to try the cod, but I've been over on the south side so I didn't see you. Why aren't you at home getting ready for tomorrow's wedding?'

'Me? I don't intend to be at the wedding,' Gusten said.

'Don't talk nonsense. Why wouldn't you be there?'

Gusten explained his reasons as best he could. He had no wish to be present at an occasion he found disgusting – and, by not being there, he would be 'pointing the finger' at someone who had done him wrong.

'And what about your mother?' the minister said. 'Don't you think it's wrong to bring shame on her?'

'I don't agree,' Gusten answered. 'What is even more wrong

is that I should get a rat like Carlsson as a stepfather and be unable to take over the farm as long as he's around.'

'Well, my boy, there's no way of changing that just now – though there may be some way in the future. So you must get in your boat early in the morning and sail home. And you are to be at the wedding!'

'Nothing's going to change my mind about that!' Gustav declared. 'My mind is made up!'

The minister dropped the subject and began eating his herrings on the hearth. 'You don't have a dram with you, do you? My old woman has taken to locking up all the strong stuff and I can't often get at it.'

Gusten did, indeed, have schnapps with him and he gave the minister a generous helping, which loosened his tongue and set him talking about parish affairs, both public and private. Sitting on the rocks outside the hut they watched the sun go down and dusk spreading a melon-coloured haze over the islands and the water. The gulls went off to rest on banks of seaweed and the crows flew towards the inner skerries to roost in the trees.

It was time for bed but first they had to drive the mosquitoes out of the hut: they shut the door and smoked the cottage full of Black Anchor tobacco, opened the door again and set about hunting with rowan switches. The two fishermen then threw off their coats and climbed into their bunks.

'You couldn't give me one last hair of the dog, could you?' the minister begged – he had already downed his fair share – and Gusten gave him the last rites there on the edge of the bed before they went to sleep.

It was dark inside the hut and only the odd streak of daylight could penetrate the cracks in the walls, but in the faint light the mosquitoes found their way to the sleepy pair, who were soon twisting and turning in their bunks to escape their tormenters.

'Oh, this is just the bloody end!' the minister groaned at last. 'Are you still asleep, Gusten?'

'Fat chance of that! Won't be much sleep here tonight, but what can we do about it?'

'We'll have to get up and light the fire – I don't see any other way. If we had a pack of cards we could play a hand. I don't suppose you have some, do you?'

'No, I don't, but I think I know where the Kvarnö boys keep theirs,' Gusten said, climbing out of bed, crawling on the floor under the bottom bunk and emerging with a rather grubby pack of cards.

The minister had started the fire, put some juniper twigs on the stove and lighted the stump of a candle. Gusten put on the coffee pot and pulled out a herring-cask, which they put between their knees as a card table. They lit their pipes, the cards were soon flying, and the hours passed.

'Draw three, pass, trump!' went the voices, interspersed with the occasional oath as a mosquito drew blood from the players' necks and knuckles.

'Listen to me now, Gusten,' the minister said at last, his mind clearly having been on things other than cards and mosquitoes. 'You can surely find some other way of putting one over on Carlsson rather than staying away from the wedding? It will just look cowardly to miss it because of a clod like him. If you really want to rattle him, I know a better way than that.'

'And how do I go about that?' asked Gusten, who did think it would be a pity to miss all the feasting since it was going to come out of his inheritance anyway.

'Arrive home in the afternoon immediately after the wedding ceremony and say that you were held up at sea. That will be insulting enough in itself, and then you and I between us will get him so drunk that he can't get into the bridal bed – and we can get all the lads to bait him about it. That will be enough, won't it?'

Gusten did not seem averse to the idea and that, along with the thought of spending three days alone on the island being eaten alive by mosquitoes every night, weakened his resolve, particularly as he really did want to be there to taste all the fine things he had seen being prepared. The minister proceeded to set out his plan of action and Gusten, who was going to collaborate in its execution, gave his approval. Pleased with themselves and with each other, they finally turned in as daylight was breaking through the cracks round the door and the mosquitoes were tiring of their nocturnal dance.

*

That same evening Carlsson heard from returning herring fishers that both Gusten and the minister had been sighted heading out for Norsten and he rightly concluded that some devilment was afoot. He had taken a strong dislike to the minister because of the six months' postponement and also because the man never tired of showing his contempt for him. Carlsson had crawled to him, prostrated himself and greased his palm, all to no avail. If they were in the same room the minister always turned his back on him, never heard anything he said and always told stories that might well be taken as applying to the current situation. So when Carlsson heard that the minister had been consorting with Gusten out in the skerries he assumed that this was a meeting with some definite purpose, and rather than simply watching and waiting for the outcome of the meeting – which he suspected would be aimed at him – he drew up a plan to nip their schemes in the bud. The bosun of the coastguards happened to be on leave and was temporarily being employed as butler and factotum on Hemsö, where his skills as an organiser of dances and the like were known and valued. In reckoning that he could rely on the bosun's cooperation to play a practical joke on the minister, Carlsson reckoned right, for the minister had once refused to allow Bosun Rapp to be confirmed on the grounds that he was too keen on the girls – and this delay of a year had caused Rapp problems in the navy. So, over coffee and a dram, these two enemies of the cloth concocted a plan to make a fool of the minister. This would inevitably necessitate the latter's over-indulgence in certain substances and there would be plenty of time and opportunity for them to ensure that would happen.

Thus the opposing sides had laid their mines and fate would decide which would produce the bigger explosion.

The day of the wedding dawned. Everyone woke tired and bad-tempered after all the fuss of preparation, and when the first guests arrived early – sea connections never being exactly precise – there was no one there to greet them and they were left to wander disconsolately around outside like gate-crashers. The bride was still not dressed and the groom was running about in his shirt-sleeves drying glasses, opening bottles and plugging candles into candlesticks. The cottage had been scrubbed and decorated with greenery and all the furniture moved out and round the back corner so that it looked as if there was to be an auction. They had erected a flagpole in the farmyard, on which they had raised the flag of the Customs Service, borrowed from the inspector for the festivities. A wreath and a crown of cowberry foliage and ox-eye daisies hung over the cottage door, on each side of which stood birch tree branches. Bottles with the brightest of coloured labels were lined up in the windows so that they gleamed through the glass like the display in a liquor store – Carlsson had a taste for gaudy effects. The golden-yellow tones of punch shone like sunbeams through the soap-green panes and the purple of the brandy glowed like a coal fire. The metal capsules covering the corks glinted like shining silver coins, tempting the bolder young farmers to approach and stare, just as if they were looking in a shop-window and anticipating the fiery pleasures that would soon scorch their gullets.

On either side of the door, like heavy mortars guarding the entrance, stood a thirty-five gallon cask, one full of schnapps and the other full of small beer. Behind them, stacked up like pyramids of cannon-balls, were two hundred bottles of beer. It was a sight of warlike splendour under the command of Bosun Rapp, who was moving round with a corkscrew swinging from his belt as he organised his military supplies. He had adorned the barrels with spruce cuttings, taken out the bungs and hammered in the metal taps, swinging his bung-hammer as if it was a ramrod and occasionally tapping the containers to let the world know there was something inside them. In his parade uniform of a blue jacket with a turned-down collar, white trousers and patent leather hat – but, for the sake of safety, minus his side-arm – he was an object of great respect among the farm-boys because, as well as being the butler, it was his job to keep order and prevent mischief, to intervene in any fights that threatened to break out and, where necessary, to throw people out. The richer lads pretended to scorn him, but that was just envy since they too would have liked to be in uniform and serving the Crown, were it not for the terror they felt at the thought of the cat-o'-nine-tails and irascible cannoneers.

Two pans of coffee were standing on the hearth in the kitchen and the borrowed coffee-grinders were rattling away. An axe had been used to break up the loaves of sugar and the buns to go with the coffee were piled on the window-sills. The maids were running back and forth to the storeroom, which was completely packed with all kinds of boiled and roast meat and sacks of freshly baked bread. Now and then the bride, her false plaits flouncing about and dressed in just her petticoat, would stick her head out of her bedroom window and yell at either Lotten or Clara.

Sail after sail could be seen steering into the bay, tacking elegantly past the end of the jetty, striking sail and coming alongside to the sound of gunshots. But the guests took their time about venturing up to the house, strolling around instead in clusters down below.

By lucky chance the professor's wife and children had been called to the mainland to celebrate a birthday and only the professor was at home. He had, therefore, not only graciously accepted an invitation to the wedding but was also allowing them to use his big drawing-room for the ceremony and his lawn under the oak-trees for the serving of coffee and supper. Long rows of planks laid on trestles and barrels had been set up to act as benches, and the tables were already covered with table-cloths and rows of coffee cups.

Small groups were now beginning to gather on the ground in front of the cottage. Rundqvist, newly shaven, with seal-oil in his hair and wearing a black jacket, had taken it upon himself to entertain the guests by making pointed remarks while Norman, who along with Rapp had been given responsibility for firing the salutes, mainly using dynamite cartridges, was round the back of the cottage rehearsing on a small scale with a pistol. In return for this honour he had been compelled to hand over his accordion, which was banned for the day since the best fiddler in the district – the tailor from Fifång – had been engaged to play and that gentleman was known to be extremely sensitive about any interference with his art.

Then the minister arrived, in a jocular wedding mood and ready, as custom required, to engage in some gentle banter with the bridal couple. Carlsson met him at the door and welcomed him.

'Well, shall we get straight to the churching?' Reverend Nordström greeted him.

'Hell, there's not that much of a hurry!' the bridegroom answered with no sign of embarrassment.

'Are you sure about that?' the minister said, needling Carlsson while the farmers stood there grinning. 'I've done the wedding, christening and churching all on the wedding day before now – mind you, they were sprightly people who knew what they were at. But more seriously, how is the bride?'

'Hm, no danger there at the moment but you can never tell once things get going,' Carlsson replied, leading him to a seat between the churchwarden's wife and the widow from Åvassa, whom the minister then proceeded to entertain with talk of the weather and the fishing.

The professor came over from his house, dressed in tails, white tie and a black top hat. The minister immediately latched on to him as a man of equal standing and started a conversation which the women – all eyes and ears – listened to intently since they were sure the professor was a man bursting with learning.

Then Carlsson came in and announced everything was ready and that they were just looking for Gusten so they could get started.

'Where is Gusten?' The call went round outside and even up in the barn.

No one answered. No one had seen him.

'Well, I know where he is!' Carlsson informed them.

'And where might that be?' the minister asked with a sly look that Carlsson did not fail to notice.

'A little bird told me he was seen out on Norsten, and there was some swine with him who probably got him drunk!'

'There's no point in waiting for him if he's fallen into bad company. It's too bad of him not to have stayed at home where there are good people to set him an example. What does the bride think? Should we get going or should we wait?'

They waited to hear the bride and she, although unhappy about it, wanted to begin because otherwise the coffee would go cold. To the sound of dynamite salutes they prepared to set off. The fiddler rosined his bow and tuned his fiddle, the minister donned his gown, the groomsmen formed an advance guard and the minister led the bride, who was dressed in black silk but with a white veil and myrtle wreath. She was so tightly corseted that everything that was meant to be concealed had become even more visible. And off they processed up to the professor's, accompanied by the screech of the fiddle and the crack of dynamite among the rocks.

Right up to the last minute the old woman was looking round anxiously for any sign of her prodigal son and as they were going through the doorway the minister was almost dragging her since she was still looking back over her shoulder. Once inside, the guests lined up round the walls as though forming the guard at an execution and the bridal couple took up their stance in front of a couple of upturned chairs that had been covered with a Brussels carpet. The minister had already produced his book, was fingering his collar bands and was about to clear his throat when the bride put a hand on his arm and asked him to wait. If they waited just a few minutes more, surely Gusten would come.

The room fell almost completely silent. The only sound to be heard was the creaking of boots and the rustle of starched skirts, and even that stopped after a few moments. People looked at one another in embarrassment, there were some dry coughs, and then silence again. Everyone's eyes were on the minister and finally he said:

'Now we'll start, otherwise we shall be waiting forever. If he's not here yet, he's not going to come.'

With that he started the service: 'Dearly beloved, Holy Matrimony, which is an honourable estate instituted of God ...'

The service had been going on for some time and the older women were sniffing at their lavender and weeping when a sudden bang was heard from outside, followed by the tinkle of breaking glass. They pricked up their ears and listened for a moment but then took no further notice – except for Carlsson, who seemed to be shuffling uneasily and sneaking glances out of the window. Then there came a fresh bang, bang, bang, like the sound of champagne corks being pulled, and the boys standing by the door began to giggle. Things were just calming down again and the minister was asking the bridegroom, 'Before Almighty God and in the presence of this congregation, wilt thou, Johannes Edvard Carlsson, take this woman, Anna Eva Flod, to thy wedded wife, to love her and comfort her in sickness and in health?' when, instead of an answer, there came a fresh and vigorous salvo of popping corks, along with the tinkling of glass – all of which set the farm dog barking furiously.

'Who on earth is opening bottles out there and disrupting the holy ceremony?' the minister roared, beside himself with rage.

'I was about to ask the same thing,' Carlsson burst out, no longer able to control his curiosity and concern. 'Is it Rapp playing the fool?'

'Hey you, what am I supposed to have done?' shouted Rapp, who was standing by the door and resented the finger being pointed at him.

Bang! Bang! Bang! The noise had now become continuous.

'In the name of Jesus, go and see that there hasn't been some kind of accident,' the minister yelled. 'We'll finish this later.'

A number of the guests rushed out, the rest crowded to the windows.

'It's the beer!' someone shouted.

'Das Bier, das Bier ... ist ... spouting!' yelled the professor.

'How could anyone be so stupid as to put beer out in the hot sun!'

The stacks of beer bottles were cracking and spluttering like machine-guns and foam was running all over the ground.

The bride was deeply upset by this unexpected interruption of the ceremony, which she felt could not augur well; the bridegroom was jeered for his bad organisation and almost came to blows with the bosun, onto whom he tried to shift the blame; the minister was angry that the bottles had disturbed the holy ceremony; but the lads stood outside drinking the dregs left in the bottoms of the bottles or accidentally happening to rescue bottles that had only blown their corks. When the storm finally settled, they assembled once more in the room, though rather less solemn than they had been, and once the minister had repeated his question to the bridegroom, the ceremony continued without any further disturbance other than that caused by the ill-concealed mirth of the boys out on the porch.

Congratulations were showered on the newly-married couple and as soon as they could they all moved outside, stinking of sweat, tears, damp stockings, lavender and withered bouquets. Then, at a rather more lively pace, they proceeded to the tables for coffee.

Carlsson took a seat between the professor and the minister but the bride had no time to sit down, having to rush here and there to oversee the arrangements.

The evening sun shone brightly and there was a hum of merry conversation under the oak trees. Once they had finished dipping their cake in their coffee, it was time for the second cup – generously laced with schnapps. But at the head of the table where the bridegroom was sitting punch was being served. Neither the farmers nor the farm-hands took this amiss, punch not being a drink that was served every day. The minister, however, was more than happy to see his cup being well-charged.

He was being unusually gentle with Carlsson today,

repeatedly toasting him, praising him and paying him a great deal of attention, though without forgetting the professor, whose acquaintance gave him all the more pleasure because he so rarely met an educated man. But he had some difficulty in finding a common interest to talk about since music was not his *forte* and because the professor, out of politeness, tried to bring the conversation round to the minister's home-ground, which was an area the latter much preferred to avoid. Moreover, their difficulty in actually understanding one another made real contact impossible, as did the fact that the professor, accustomed as he was to expressing himself through music, did not enjoy engaging in long conversations.

Then the fiddler, who found it intolerable that so little attention was being paid to him, came up to the top of the table and, with his courage considerably boosted by his intake of laced coffee, wanted to discuss music with the professor.

'Pardon me, Mr Conductor, sir,' he said by way of greeting, plucking his fiddle at the same time, 'we've sort of got something in common, because I play too, I do, in my own way of course.'

'Why don't you go to Hell, tailor!' Carlsson snarled. 'Don't be so impertinent!'

'Oh yes, I do beg your pardon, sir – not that it's any business of Carlsson's – but just feel this fiddle, sir, just feel it and see if it isn't a good one. I bought it at Hirsch's and it cost me not a penny less than fifteen daler.'

The professor plucked the E-string and said graciously:

'Verry wunderbar!'

'You see! At last someone who knows what he's talking about! Now we get the truth! Unlike talking about Art with these ... with these bloody peasants here!' He had meant to say this *sotto voce* but his vocal equipment refused all nuancing and it emerged as a shout instead.

'Someone give that tailor a kick up the backside!' the bloody peasants chorused.

'Don't you dare get drunk, tailor, we want to do some dancing later!'

'Rapp, keep an eye on the fiddler. Make sure he doesn't have any more to drink.'

'I was invited here with the offer of free drinks! But you're getting tight-fisted, now, are you, you miser?'

'Just sit down, Fredrik, and keep quiet,' the minister said, 'otherwise someone is going to thump you!'

The fiddler, however, was absolutely set on discussing his 'Art' and in order to illustrate the quality he claimed for his instrument he began doodling away on it.

'Listen to that, sir, listen to those bass notes. Don't they just sound like a little organ?'

'Can't someone shut the tailor up!'

There was movement round the tables and the levels of intoxication were increasing but then someone shouted, 'Gusten is here!'

'Where? Where is he?'

Clara told them she had seen him down by the wood-pile.

'Let me know when he comes in,' the minister said. 'But not before he is actually in, do you hear me?'

The toddy glasses were now produced and Rapp was opening bottles of brandy.

'This is all going a bit too fast,' the minister said, about to decline a glass. Carlsson, however, thought everything was going to plan.

Rapp, meanwhile, went round quietly encouraging everyone to toast the minister, who had soon downed his first toddy and had to top up his glass with the second.

The minister began to roll his eyes and chew, attempting to focus as closely as he could on Carlsson's face in order to decide whether he had received his just deserts yet. But he had trouble seeing him and had to confine himself to drinking a toast with him instead.

Then Clara came in and shouted:

'He's inside now, reverend, he's inside now!'

'What the hell are you talking about, girl? Inside ... who's inside?' the minister said, having forgotten who they were talking about.

'Which who is inside, Clara?' they all chorused.

'Gusten, of course!'

The minister got up, went into the cottage and fetched a shy and confused-looking Gusten, whom he led back to the table and made everyone greet with a cup of punch and a cheer. Then Gusten drank a toast with Carlsson and said quickly, 'Good luck, then!'

Carlsson became sentimental at this, downed what was in his glass and announced what a great pleasure it was to see him – even though he was late – and that he knew two people whose old hearts would rejoice at the sight of him – even though he was late.

'And believe me,' he concluded, 'anyone who knows how to take old Carlsson in the right way, knows where he stands with him'.

Gusten was not exactly carried away by this speech but he invited Carlsson to drink a special glass with him, just the two of them.

The evening was now drawing in, the mosquitoes were dancing and conversation was buzzing. There was the chink of glasses, there were peals of laughter and from here and there in the bushes came – already – little shrieks for help, interrupted by giggles and cheers, yells and gunshots, all under the warm sky of a summer's evening. Out in the meadows the crickets chirped and the corncrakes rasped.

The tables were cleared since it was now time to lay them for supper. Rapp went round hanging Chinese lanterns he had borrowed from the professor in the branches of the oak trees, Norman ran round with piles of plates and Rundqvist was down on his knees tapping the small beer and schnapps. The girls carried out mounds of butter, piles of herring on wooden platters, stacks of pancakes and heaps of meatballs. When it was all ready, the bridegroom clapped his hands:

'Come and have something to eat – you're all very welcome.'

'Where's the minister?' some of the older women asked in servile tones. No one would start without the minister.

'And the professor? Where have they gone? We really can't

start without them.'

They shouted and they searched, but all in vain. They stood round the tables like packs of hungry dogs, eyes gleaming and ready to leap in, but no one would budge and the silence was becoming oppressive.

'Mm, I wonder, maybe the minister has, um, gone to the you-know-where?' Rundqvist suggested, all innocence.

Without waiting for further information Carlsson set off down to the privy and, sure enough, there sat the minister and the professor – door wide open, newspapers in hand – engaged in a lively discussion. The lantern was down on the floor and it was casting a glow like footlights up at the two men on their thrones.

'Excuse me, gentlemen, but the food's going cold!'

'Is that you, Carlsson? I see, I see! You just get started and we'll be with you straightaway.'

'Yes, but everyone's standing waiting, everyone – and with respect, sirs, if you could perhaps just hurry up a bit.'

'Coming at once, coming at once! Away with you now, away!'

Carlsson, who had noticed with great satisfaction that the minister seemed 'emotional', left them and hurried back to set the assembled minds at rest and to pass on the news that the minister was just doing his business and would be with them presently.

A moment later a lantern, followed by two unsteady shadows, was to be seen meandering up the slope and approaching the supper tables.

The minister's pale face soon appeared at the head of the table and the bride stepped forward with the bread basket to put an end to the embarrassing delay. Carlsson, however, had something else in mind and after rapping the meatball dish with his knife he called in a loud voice:

'Quiet, my good people, quiet! The minister would like to say a few words.'

The minister stared at Carlsson and seemed to have no idea where he was. Noticing that he was holding something shiny, he remembered that he had given a speech last Christmas with a silver cup in his hand, so he raised the lantern as if it were a goblet and began:

'My friends, we are here today to celebrate a joyous occasion.'

At this point he stared at Carlsson, trying to get some idea of the nature and purpose of the joyous occasion since he was now completely at a loss – season, place, reason, purpose had all deserted him. But Carlsson's grinning face offered him no solution to the mystery. He stared out into space looking for a clue, saw the Chinese lanterns in the oak trees and got a swaying image of an enormous Christmas tree, which set him on the right track.

'This happy festival of light,' he began, 'when the sun has given way to the cold and when the snow ...' He looked at the white table tablecloth as if it was a great snowfield stretching away into an infinite distance. 'My friends, when the first snow settles like a blanket over the dirt of autumn ... no, no, I think you're all laughing at me! Urgh!!'

He suddenly turned his back on them and doubled up.

'I think the minister's feeling the cold,' Carlsson said, 'and he'd like to go and lie down! Please just tuck in, ladies and gentlemen!'

There was no need to ask them twice and leaving the minister to his fate they set about demolishing the laden dishes.

The minister had been given the professor's attic bedroom as accommodation for the night and in an attempt to demonstrate his sobriety he rejected all offers of assistance with threats of violence. With the lantern hanging down by his knees and bent over as if he was looking for needles in the dewy grass, he set his course by a window in which there was a light. He got stuck in the gateway, however, and banged into the gatepost so violently that his light went out and the lantern was smashed. Darkness closed around him like a sack and he sank to his knees, but the lighted window guided him like a beacon and he thought he was making progress, though he had an uneasy feeling that the knees of his black trousers were becoming wetter with every step and his kneecaps were as painful as if they were striking stone.

Finally he managed to get hold of something very big, round and damp. He fumbled about, pricking himself on something that felt like a needle-case, getting his hand stuck in a rowlock or something of the sort, heard a sudden rushing of water and realised he was getting wet. Terrified by the thought he had walked into the sea, he pulled himself up on the mast and found, in a sudden moment of clarity, that he was standing by a door-post, then he heeled over into the hallway, felt his knees in contact with a staircase and heard a maid scream: 'Jesus, the small beer!' Driven on by a vague sense of bad conscience he crawled up the stairs, banged his knuckles on a key, managed to open a door that went inwards and saw a large bed, all made up and with space for two. He had just enough strength to pull back the covers, get in with his boots and everything else on, and hide himself from the yells that were pursuing him from downstairs. And then he thought he died or was extinguished or drowned to the sound of people shouting about small beer. Now and then he came back to life, flickered awake, was dragged out of the sea to stand before the Christmas table, but then he was blown out again like a candle, doused, died, sank and felt himself getting wet.

Meanwhile, down under the oaks, supper was going on, washed down with such quantities of beer and schnapps that no one remembered the minister, and once they had galloped their way through all the food so that the bottoms of the dishes and plates were gleaming and bare, they all went down to the cottage to dance.

The bride wanted to send something tasty up to the minister's bedroom but Carlsson convinced her that he would rather be left in peace and it would be a pity to embarrass him. So they left it at that.

Gusten had deserted his ally when he saw him being outwitted and was devoting himself instead to his own pleasures, his rancour and grudges submerged in boozy oblivion.

The dancing was pounding along like a mill and the fiddler, ensconced by the fireplace, was sawing away at his fiddle.

Sweaty backs leaned out of the open windows to enjoy the cool of the fresh night air and the older guests were sitting out on the green smoking, drinking, cheering when shots were fired and having fun in the half-dusk and what light seeped through the windows from the kitchen fire and the candles in the dancing room.

Out in the meadows and among the hillocks, however, couple after couple strolled through the dewy grass by the faint twinkling light of the starry sky and, to the song of the crickets among the scented hay, sought to quench the fires kindled by the heat of the cottage, the spirit of the barley and the rhythmic pulse of the music.

The midnight hours danced past and the sky in the east began to grow lighter. The stars retreated into the heavens and the Plough stood on end with its shaft in the air as if it had tipped over backwards. Down among the reeds the ducks began quacking and the smooth waters of the bay reflected the lemon colours of the dawn sky between the dark shapes of the alder trees, which seemed to be standing on their heads in the water and reaching down to touch the bottom. But it only lasted a moment before clouds drifted up from the coast and night returned.

Then there was a sudden cry from the kitchen, 'Glögg! Glögg!' and in processed the men bearing a cauldron of flaming schnapps, its flames casting a blue light all round as the fiddler played a march.

'Up to the minister with the first glass!' Carlsson yelled, hoping to give the *coup de grâce* to his opponent, and his suggestion was welcomed with cheers. The procession set off up to the professor's house and clambered – more or less steadily – up the stairs to the attic. The key was in the door and in they tramped, a touch fearful that they would be met with a shower of blows. The room was silent and in the trembling blue light from the cauldron they could see that the bed was empty and untouched. A dark premonition of some ghastly reversal seized Carlsson but he hid his suspicions and, to quell the uncertainties and guesses of the others, he concocted the explanation that he had just remembered the minister saying he would sleep in the hayloft to escape the mosquitoes. Since no one was allowed anywhere near the hay with naked lights, they could not go there and the procession set off back to the green where the sacrifice was performed.

Carlsson quickly appointed Gusten as his deputy host, took Rapp to one side and shared his dreadful suspicions with him. Then the two companions in crime crept unnoticed up the stairs to the bridal chamber, taking matches and a candle stump with them.

Rapp struck a light and there in the bridal bed Carlsson saw all his worst fears exceeded.

A head as shaggy as a wet dog's, mouth wide-open, lay on the white hemstitched pillow.

'Can you bloody believe it!' Carlsson hissed. 'Who'd have thought that bugger could be such a pig? God have mercy on us! And the swine's got his boots on too!'

This was going to take some thinking about! How to get the sick man out of there without disturbing him, without the guests knowing about it and, above all, without the bride finding out?

'We'll have to take him out of the window,' Rapp suggested. 'We'll have to use a block and tackle – and then we'll drag him down to the shore. Put the light out and we'll go and get the gear from the barn.'

They locked the door from the outside and, taking the key with them, the two avengers set off on a roundabout route to the barn, Carlsson cursing and swearing that if they could just get him out of there they would really put him to shame afterwards.

Luckily for them the shear-legs were still standing in the barn after the slaughter of the cow and once they had separated the struts and found the block and tackle they made their way back by a circuitous path behind the cottage and reached the gable-end under the minister's window. Rapp fetched a ladder and erected the shear-legs, securing them to a lath near the ridge of the roof. Then he spliced a strap, fixed the block and mounted the tackle. After that he slipped into the bedroom while Carlsson stood down below with a boat-hook, ready to fend off.

Rapp, with much puffing and panting, had been busy in the bedroom for some time before Carlsson saw his head stick out of the window and quietly give the order to haul.

Carlsson duly hauled and a dark shape soon emerged on the window-sill.

'Haul hard!' Rapp ordered, and Carlsson heaved. The minister's slack body, incredibly elongated like that of a hanged man, was now dangling from the shear-legs.

'Lower away!' Rapp ordered. 'No, hold fast a moment!'

But Carlsson had already let go and the minister was lying in a heap in the nettles, still without uttering a sound.

The bosun was out through the window in a flash and removed the ladder and the shear-legs. Then they dragged the minister down to the jetty.

'Now, you bugger, time for you to have a bath!' Carlsson snapped once they had reached the water's edge.

The water was shallow but oozing with slime from all the fish-guts that had been thrown in over the years. Rapp took hold of the strap he had fastened round the sleeping minister and hurled him into the sea.

At last, with a scream like a pig being slaughtered, the minister woke.

'Heave!' ordered Rapp, who had seen that the people up on the green had noticed something was going on and were already hurrying towards them.

Carlsson, however, knelt down and rolled the minister in the sludge, rubbing it into his black clothes with his hands so that every trace of the accident that had happened in the bridal bed was scrubbed away.

'What's going on down there? What's happening?' shouted the men as they came rushing down to the water's edge.

'Ahoy there! The minister's fallen in the sea!' Rapp answered as he heaved the yelling minister ashore.

Everyone clustered around, Carlsson playing the Good

Samaritan, the noble rescuer who had saved the minister from mortal danger. He turned his eyes to the heavens and lamented in the broken dialect he always put on when he wanted to sound sympathetic and sincere.

'Can you believe it! It was pure chance that I comes down here and then I hears something splashing and snuffling and thinks it's a seal – but then I sees that it's our own dear minister. Lord Above, I says to the bosun, I do believe it's the Rev. Nordström himself, lying there waving his little flippers. So I says to Rapp – Rapp, I says, run and get some rope and Rapp runs to get some rope. But when we gets the rope round his middle he starts yelling and screaming as if we was trying to geld him. And just look at the state he's in.'

The minister did, indeed, look indescribable. The men looked at the shepherd of their souls with disgust, but the unshakeable respect they felt for him made them want to remove him from the public gaze as quickly as possible. They fashioned a stretcher from two pairs of oars, laid the minister on it and, carried on eight strong shoulders, he was taken up to the barn to have his clothes changed.

The fiddler, who was completely drunk and thought this was all part of the show, swung his bow and struck up the tune 'Make way! Make way for old Smitten's bier!' The boys emerged from the bushes and joined the procession; the professor, who had rediscovered his lost youth, walked in front and sang; and Norman, unable to resist the temptation to indulge in musical effusions any longer, had managed to find his accordion.

When they reached the yard the women came rushing out, and when they saw the grievous state of the minister they were overcome by sympathy and compassion for the poor unconscious fellow. In spite of Carlsson's warnings the old woman ran to fetch a bedspread to cover the distressing sight while they put water on to heat and borrowed linen and clothes from the professor. Once in the barn the sick man – as they called him, since no one wanted to be so disrespectful as to suggest he was drunk – was placed on dry straw. Rundqvist produced his lancet and wanted to bleed him but they chased him away, and since he was not allowed to do that he asked permission to say a spell over him – he claimed to know a spell that worked on sheep suffering from dropsy. The women, however, refused to let either Rundqvist or any of the other men come anywhere near the minister.

Carlsson, meanwhile, crept up to the bridal bedroom, alone this time, to clear up the traces of his humiliation. When he went in and saw the fouling and the desecration of the bridal bed and the devastation that had been wreaked on it, he was overcome with weakness for a moment, exhausted by the travails of the last days and nights. He thought how different it would all have been with Ida if their relationship had come to pass. He walked over to the window and looked out over the bay with a heavy heart. The clouds had dispersed and mist was gathering like a white veil over the water. The sun was rising and it broke through into the bridal chamber, shining on his pallid face and washed-out eyes, which were closed tight as though he were fighting to hold back tears. His hair hung down in damp tufts over his forehead, his white neckerchief was streaked with dirt and his coat hung loose on him. The warmth of the sun seemed to give him a fit of the shivers and, wiping his brow with his hand, he turned back into the room.

'What a disaster, what an absolute disaster!' he said to himself. Then he shook off his lethargy and began stripping the bed.

CHAPTER VI

*Circumstances change and opinions change; agriculture declines
and quarrying flourishes.*

Carlsson was not the man to let unpleasant experiences
affect him more than he chose to – he had the strength to
take the knocks, shake himself and fight on. He had won his
position as owner of the farm as a result of his knowledge and
competence and, in his opinion, when Madame Flod took him
as her husband she benefited at least as much as he did. Once
the smoke of the wedding had dispersed, however, he began
to be less keen: he was, after all, now secure both in his marital
portion and his inheritance rights, all the more so since a baby
was expected in a few months. He had given up the idea of
behaving as the laird when he saw that it would not work and,
instead, set about playing the part of the gentleman farmer.
He took to wearing a splendid woollen jersey, a huge leather
apron and sea-boots. He spent much of his time sitting at the
bureau – his favourite place – reading the newspaper rather
than writing and doing the accounts as he had done in the
past. He supervised the work with his pipe in his mouth and
took less and less interest in working the land.

'Farming's on the decline,' he said, 'it says so in the paper. It's
cheaper to buy corn.'

'That's not what you said before,' Gusten answered. He had
been keeping a close eye on everything Carlsson said and
did at the same time as behaving with a kind of apathetic
submissiveness that fell well short of accepting any family
relationship with the intruder.

'Times change and we must change with them! I thank the

Lord that I get wiser with every passing day!' Carlsson replied.

Carlsson also began to attend church on Sundays, involved himself in public affairs and was elected to the local council. This brought him into closer contact with the minister and eventually the great day dawned when he was permitted to drop the minister's title and call him by name. This was a dream come true for Carlsson, the achievement of one of his greatest ambitions, and for the next year he never tired of telling the people on the farm what he had said to the minister and what the minister had answered.

'"Now you listen to me, Nordström, my dear chap," I said, "this time you should let me be the one to decide". And then Nordström said, "Carlsson," he said, "you're a smart fellow and a sensible fellow, but you shouldn't be so stubborn," he said.'

A number of communal responsibilities followed, his favourite being fire inspection since it meant travelling around at the expense of the parish and drinking coffee and schnapps with acquaintances. The parliamentary election, too, although it took place away over on the mainland, had its attractions and its small perks that made themselves felt even out in the skerries. At election time, and on one or two other occasions during the year, the baron would come out by steamer with a party of hunting guests and they would pay fifty kronor for a couple of days' hunting rights. Punch and brandy would flow all day and all night and when the hunters departed they left behind them a real sense of having been 'proper gentry'.

Carlsson, then, was going up in the world, was a guiding light on the farm, an authority with superior knowledge of things the others did not understand. But there was one weak point remaining and there were times when he really felt it: coming from the mainland as he did, he was no seaman.

In order to make good this last shortcoming he began to immerse himself more and more in maritime matters and to show an increased enthusiasm for the sea. He polished up a gun and went hunting, took part in seine-netting and sweep-netting and even ventured out on lengthy sailing trips.

'Agriculture's on the decline and we must push the fishing,' he answered his wife when she expressed concern about his neglect of the beasts and the fields.

'Fishing first and fishing foremost! Fish for the fisherman and land for the farmer!' he proclaimed, irresistible now that the schoolmaster had taught him how to use 'parlamentry rettorick' at parish council meetings.

When the flow of cash began to fall off, Carlsson set them all to chopping wood.

'The woods need thinning out to let the timber mature! That's what these rational agriculturalists are saying anyway – not that I would know, of course!'

And if Carlsson did not know, how could anyone else know?

The farming was left in Rundqvist's hands, the cattle in Clara's. Rundqvist sowed the arable fields with grass, snoozed away the morning on the banks around the fields and then snoozed until supper-time in the bushes. When the cows refused to give milk, he fell back on his spells and passed steel across their backs.

Gusten spent even more time at sea than before and renewed his old hunting partnership with Norman. And so the common interest that had kept them all working together for a while ebbed away: there was no real pleasure to be found in working for others and, calmly and quietly, things began to go to the dogs.

Towards autumn, however, a couple of months after the wedding, there was an event that hit Carlsson's ship, sailing as it was under full sail, with the force of a sudden squall: the child his wife was expecting arrived very prematurely and stillborn. The circumstances, moreover, were of such concern that the doctor declared emphatically that this was to be the end of it: she was to have no more children.

This was a calamity for Carlsson, who could see his future prospects shrinking to the point where he would be left with little more than maintenance rights, and given the delicate state of his wife's health following her confinement this change in his status was threatening to occur earlier than could have been envisaged. It was essential, then, for him to use the time profitably, to cosy up to an unjust Mammon, to gather corn into his granary and think of the morrow.

Carlsson came to life again. Farming was now to be given priority, and quickly. Why? That was nobody's business! Timber was felled so that a new cottage could be built. Why? No reason to justify it to them! Norman's hunting bug had to be crushed at once, so he was seduced away from his friend Gusten yet again. Rundqvist was snared by increasing his benefits. They ploughed, sowed, fished and built, and all Carlsson's communal duties were pushed to one side.

At the same time Carlsson began to focus on domestic life and took to devoting much time to sitting with the old woman, sometimes even reading to her from Holy Scripture or from the hymn book, appealing to her heart and nobler sentiments without rightly being able to explain where he was going with it. The old woman enjoyed the company and having a voice to listen to, so she valued these small marks of attention without being particularly concerned about the possible implications of these preparations for departure from this world.

One winter's evening the people of Hemsö – Gusten among them – were gathered together in the kitchen. The inlet was frozen, the bays impassable and they had been cut off for a fortnight, unable to visit neighbours or receive letters or newspapers; snow and isolation were weighing heavily on them and the days were too short to allow much meaningful work. The fire was burning in the stove and the men were making nets, the girls spinning and Rundqvist was whittling away at spade handles. Snow had been falling all day and was already above the window-panes so the kitchen had the feel of a room in which a corpse has been laid out. Every quarter of an hour one of the men had to go out and shovel the snow away from the door to prevent them being snowed in and unable to reach the byre to milk the cows or give them fodder for the night.

It was Gusten's turn to go out with the shovel this time and, donning oilskins and a sou'wester over his jersey and otter-fur cap, he heaved open the front door, against which drifts had built up, and went out into the whirling snow. The air was dark and snowflakes as grey as moths and big as hens' feathers were spinning ceaselessly down and ceaselessly and silently landing on top of one another, lightly at first but then more heavily as they compacted and grew deeper. The drifts already reached a good way up the walls of the cottage and it was only through the upper edge of the windows that the light from inside showed through. Gusten noticed that there was light coming from the parlour, where he knew Carlsson was sitting with his mother, and in a sudden fit of curiosity he poked a peephole through the upper snow, climbed up on the snowdrift and looked in. Carlsson, as usual, was sitting at the open bureau and in front of him was a large sheet of paper stamped at the top with a big blue seal that made it closely resemble the design on the notes of the national bank. With his pen raised ready for action he was sitting beside his wife talking to her and he seemed to be on the point of handing her the pen for her to sign something. Gusten put his ear to the window-pane but could hear no more than a murmur of voices through the double windows. He was, however, very keen to know what was going on since he suspected it would concern him more than anyone else – and he had learnt that transactions signed on stamped paper were likely to be important.

He carefully opened the porch door, kicked off his straw over-shoes and crept up the stairs until he reached the landing. By lying on his stomach and hanging his head over the edge just above the door of the parlour he could hear what was being said in there.

'Anna Eva,' Carlsson was proclaiming, in a voice somewhere between that of a hawker of religious tracts and that of a parish councillor, 'Anna Eva, life is short and death may come upon us before we know it. We must, therefore, be mindful of our going hence – be it today or be it tomorrow is as one. Sign, therefore – as well to sign now as later!'

The old woman did not enjoy listening to all this talk of death but Carlsson had talked of nothing else for months so she was unable to put up more than a feeble resistance to his proposal.

'You do see, don't you, Carlsson, that dying sooner or later, today or in ten years time, is not one and the same thing to me. I may live for ages yet.'

'Indeed! And I'm not saying you *will* die, I'm just saying that we *may* die and, since it's going to happen anyway, it makes no difference whether it happens tomorrow or in ten years' time. Now, just put your signature there!'

'But I don't understand,' his wife continued to resist, just as if death were standing waiting for her. 'It surely can't ...'

'Yes, but it makes no difference since it's going to happen anyway! But maybe that's not how it is! I don't know, I just don't know! Just sign it anyway.'

Carlsson's 'I don't know, I just don't know' was as good as a noose tightening round her neck; the old woman could not hold out any longer and began to give way.

'Well, so where do we go from here?' she asked, exhausted and bored by the long discussion.

'You must think of those who come after you, Anna Eva, that is everyone's first duty. And that's why you should sign it.'

At that moment the kitchen door opened and Clara called out for Gusten who, not wanting to give himself away, kept quiet, but it meant that he was unable to hear the rest of what was said in the parlour.

Clara went back in and Gusten climbed down. He stopped outside the door of the parlour, however, and heard Carlsson's final words, which were enough for him to conclude that a will had been drawn up and that his mother had signed it.

When he went back into the kitchen, the others could see that something was not right. He talked in mysterious terms of shooting a fox he had heard barking, that it would be better to go to sea than to stay at home being eaten alive by lice, that old nags could be livened up by adding just a little white powder to their fodder – but a little bit too much could kill them!

Carlsson, on the other hand, was all smiles at the supper table, inquiring about Gusten's plans for work and for hunting. He took out the hour-glass and let the white sand trickle through it because, he said, 'minutes are precious things: let us eat and drink for tomorrow we die! With a Heigh and a Ho and a Nonny-nonny No!'

That night Gusten lay awake for a long time with a mixture of dark thoughts and darker plans running through his head, but he lacked the force of character to alter circumstances at will or to turn his thoughts into action; instead, once he had thought a thing through he would put it aside as if it was then all done and dusted.

After he had slept for a couple of hours, dreaming of other things, his cheerful mood was restored and he reckoned it would all turn out well in the end, the day would provide the answers, justice would duly take its course, and so on and so on.

*

It was spring again, the swallows mended their nests and the professor returned.

In his time on the island Carlsson had cleared the ground for a garden round the cottage, in which he planted lilacs from shoots and cuttings he had got from the manse, as well as fruit trees and fruit bushes, and he had laid out sandy paths and built arbours. The farm was beginning to look like a country estate and there was no denying that the incomer had brought comfort and prosperity with him, cultivating the fields and tending the beasts properly and maintaining the buildings and the fences. He had even succeeded in pushing up the price they got for their fish and had come to an arrangement with the steamer so that it was no longer necessary to make the long and time-consuming journeys to town.

But now that he was beginning to get tired and to ease off – and was spending his time building his new cottage – people began to moan.

'Have a go yourselves and see how well you get on!' Carlsson retorted. 'Every man for himself and may God be with us all!'

He already had the roof on his cottage and had started

laying out a garden there too, clearing the ground, laying paths and planting. He had shown a sense of style in the building of the cottage and it put the others to shame: although it only had two rooms and a kitchen downstairs it somehow looked grander than the older cottages on the farm, though quite why was impossible to say. Perhaps it was because he had raised the roof-beams a little higher and made the eaves project farther from the walls; or perhaps it was because he had sawn cross-patterns in the roofing boards; or possibly it was the veranda in front of the front door, with steps leading up to it. Whatever it was – and it was not a case of extravagance – it all managed to have the look of a villa rather than a cottage. It was painted as red as a cow but the butt-ends of the corner timbers were weather-boarded and painted black. The window-ledges were white and the veranda, which had a light roof supported by four poles, was painted blue. Carlsson had also chosen the site judiciously – right under the rocky hillock and with two old oaks growing in front of it like the start of a planned avenue or park. The view from the veranda could not have been more beautiful: the reedy bay, the long green meadow and the shallow dip that ran through the cattle pasture and allowed a sight of the boats far out in the sound.

Gusten wandered round glaring at all this, willing it to be undone. He watched it all as he would watch a wasp in the process of building a nest under the rafters, wanting to tear it down before the pest had time to lay eggs and take up residence with its offspring. But he was not up to taking on Carlsson, who consequently carried on regardless.

The old woman was in poor health and thought that everything was as it should be: Carlsson was, when all was said and done, her husband and, anticipating the turmoil that would break out when she went the way of all flesh, she was not displeased to see that he would have a roof over his head rather than end up on the parish. Her understanding of legal matters was weak though she had a vague feeling that the business of the inventory, the division of property and the will was to some degree suspect, but that was a matter for later and she hoped not to have anything to do with it. One day, however, it was all going to blow up in their faces – on the day Gusten thought of getting married for instance, if not before, and someone must have been putting thoughts of that kind in his mind since he was not his old self these days and went around looking moody.

One afternoon at the end of May Carlsson was at work walling in the stove in his new kitchen when Clara appeared and shouted to him:

'Carlsson, Carlsson, the professor's here with a German gentleman who's looking for you!'

Carlsson whipped off his leather apron, dried his hands and tidied himself up for a visitor, curious as to the cause of this unexpected visit.

Out on the veranda he found the professor in the company of a canny-looking gentleman with a long black beard.

'Ah Carlsson,' the professor said, gesturing towards his companion, 'Director Diethoff would like a word with you'.

Carlsson brushed off the seats on the bench on the veranda and invited them to sit down.

But the director did not have time to sit down and, standing where he was, asked whether Rågholmen was for sale.

Carlsson inquired why, Rågholmen being a tiny island of scarcely three acres, consisting of rocky outcrops, a few spruce trees and no more than an insignificant amount of grazing for sheep.

'For industrial purposes,' the director stated before going on to ask what the price might be.

Carlsson was at a loss and asked for time to think it over – he needed time to work out what made the island so unexpectedly valuable. But the director had no intention of giving Carlsson time to find out and, instead, repeated his question about how much it would cost at the same time as putting his hand over his breast pocket, where a thick bulge visible through the material hinted that they were not talking about pennies!

'I can't imagine it's going to be too much,' Carlsson said, 'but I'll have to talk to my wife and stepson first.'

He ran down to the cottage and was away for some time before returning.

He looked rather embarrassed and seemed to have some difficulty in voicing his suggestion.

'Well now, sir, perhaps you could say what you're prepared to offer?'

No, the director would not do that.

'Well, if I were to say five, you wouldn't think it was too much, I hope,' Carlsson managed to blurt out, breathless and with sweat breaking out on his forehead.

Director Diethoff opened his coat, took out his wallet and counted out ten one-hundred krona notes.

'Right, here's the first thousand down and the other four will be paid in the autumn. Is that acceptable?'

Carlsson very nearly put his foot in it at this point but, managing to control the flood of emotions that almost overwhelmed him, responded calmly that it was acceptable: his *five* had meant five hundred but he was getting it in thousands. They then went down to the cottage for Madame Carlsson and her son to sign the contract of sale and give the director a receipt for the sum. Carlsson winked and made faces at Gusten and his mother to get them to go along with him but they had no idea what he meant.

At last, after the contract was signed, the old woman put on her glasses and read it.

'Five thousand!' she shrieked. 'What in Heaven's name ... Carlsson, you said five hundred!'

'Really? You must have heard wrong, Anna Eva. I said thousand, didn't I, Gusten?' Carlsson said, winking at Gusten so ferociously that the director noticed.

'I was absolutely sure you said thousand!' Gusten said, supporting him as well as he could.

With the signing completed the director revealed that he and his company were intending to quarry feldspar on Rågholmen.

None of them knew what feldspar was and none of them had ever thought of such a treasure – apart from Carlsson, of course, who managed to imply that he had had his own thoughts in that direction but lacked the capital to do anything about it.

The director then explained to them that feldspar was a red mineral used in the manufacture of porcelain. The manager's house, already ordered from the joiner's, would be put up within a week and a wooden hut to house thirty workers would be in place within a fortnight, and then work could start.

With that the director departed.

This shower of gold poured down on them so suddenly that they had no time to consider all the consequences. A thousand kronor on the table and a further four thousand in the autumn, all for a worthless skerry – it was too much to take in all at once. They spent the whole evening speculating amicably about the incidental advantages that might come their way. They would, of course, be able to sell fish and other produce to the manager and all his workers – wood, too, there was no doubt about that. And then the director would visit, possibly bringing his family, and want to rent a place for the summer, which would mean that they could raise the professor's rent, and Carlsson's cottage could also be let to someone. Everything was going to be wonderful.

Carlsson put the money in the bureau himself and sat there half the night working on figures.

*

During the following week Carlsson made frequent trips to Dalarö, returning with carpenters and painters and holding small meetings on his veranda, where he had put out a table at which he sat drinking brandy and smoking his pipe as he supervised the work, which was now proceeding full speed ahead.

Soon all the rooms had been wallpapered, including the kitchen, where a Bolinder stove had been built in; the outside of the windows had been fitted with green shutters that shone even at a distance; the veranda had been repainted white and rose-coloured and an awning of blue and white striped bedticking erected on the sunny side; a picket fence, painted grey but with white knobs, ran all the way round the yard and garden. People stood for hours gaping at all this splendour but Gusten kept his distance, hiding round the corner of the house or concealed behind a thick bush and seldom or never accepting an invitation to Carlsson's veranda.

One of Carlsson's dreams, a dream he only had on really clear nights, was to sit on the veranda like the professor, leaning back self-indulgently, sipping from a brandy glass with a stem, looking at the view and smoking a pipe – ideally it would be a cigar but that was perhaps going a bit too far as yet.

And that is how he was sitting early one morning a week later when he heard a steamer blow its whistle in the sound off Rågholmen.

'Here they come,' he thought, and as master of the place he wanted to do the courteous thing and welcome them.

He went down to the cottage and got dressed, then sent for Rundqvist and Norman to accompany him out to Rågholmen to greet the strangers.

Half an hour later the boat put out from the harbour with Carlsson sitting at the helm and reminding the men every now and then to keep stroke with each other so their arrival would make a smart impression.

As they rounded the last headland and the sound opened out in front with Storön to one side of them and Rågholmen to the other, a magnificent spectacle came into view. A steamer decorated with pennants and signal flags was anchored in the sound and small jolly boats crewed by sailors in blue and white jerseys were passing between ship and shore. Standing up on the cliff, which shone rosy and red with exposed feldspar, was a cluster of gentlemen and a short distance away from them stood a brass band, its instruments gleaming against the black of the spruce trees.

The oarsmen from Hemsö wondered what on earth was going on and rowed under the shelter of the cliff to get as close as possible in order to watch and listen. Then, without warning, just as they rowed in below the meeting place, there came a swishing through the air as if a thousand eider duck had taken off at the same time, followed by a roar that seemed to come from within the cliff itself and a crash as if the whole island was splitting apart.

'What the Hell ...' was all Carlsson managed to say before a hail of rocks splashed down round the boat, followed by a rain of gravel and a shower of grit.

A voice up on the cliff-top began making a speech, talking of great industries and trades and accumulated labour, before finishing with something in a foreign language that the Hemsö men could not understand.

Rundqvist thought it must be a preacher and removed his cap but Carlsson realised it was the director speaking.

'Yes, gentlemen,' the director said, finishing his speech, 'we see many stones here before us and I conclude by expressing the hope that they may all be turned into bread!'

'Hurrah!'

The band began playing a march and the gentlemen processed down to the shore, all of them carrying pieces of rock that they fingered and fiddled with amid laughter and joking.

'Hey, you there, you in the boat! What are you up to?' shouted a gentleman in naval uniform at the Hemsö men, who were resting on their oars.

They had no idea how to respond, not having thought there might be anything wrong with watching the ceremony.

'Ah! But here is Mr Carlsson himself, I do believe,' Director Diethoff informed them, stepping forward. 'He's our landlord here,' he said by way of introduction. 'Come and join us for breakfast!'

Carlsson could not believe his ears, but they assured him that the invitation was a genuine one and showed him to a seat at a table on the after-deck of the steamer. He had never seen anything like it. At first he felt embarrassed and self-conscious but the gentlemen were extraordinarily affable and would not even let him remove his leather apron. Rundqvist and Norman, however, had to eat up in the bows with the crew.

Carlsson had never dreamt that paradise could be so wonderful. Foods he did not know the names of but which melted in his mouth like honey, foods that burned the throat just like a dram, foods of every colour imaginable. Six glasses stood lined up in front of his place – in front of all the other gentlemen, too – and they drank wines that were like smelling a flower or kissing a girl, wines that caught in his nose, wines that made his legs tingle and others that made him want to laugh. All the while the band was playing music so sweet that the corners of his eyes filled as though he was about to weep, or his temples shivered as if he was cold, or his whole body felt so glorious that he wanted to die there and then.

When it came to an end the director gave a speech in honour of their landlord, lauding him for bringing honour to his class and for not deserting the primary industries to make uncertain profits in other areas, where poverty might walk arm in arm with luxury. Then they all drank a toast to him. Much of the time Carlsson had no idea when to laugh or when to be serious but, on seeing the other gentlemen laughing at something he thought had been serious, he joined in the laughter.

Coffee and cigars were to be served after breakfast and they all rose from the table. Carlsson, feeling as magnanimous as only a happy man can, was going forward to check that his men had been given a bite to eat when the director called him and asked him to step into the cabin for a moment.

Once in the cabin Herr Diethoff put it to him that in order to consolidate his status and to be in a position, were it called for, to act with more authority among the workers on Rågholmen, he should subscribe to some shares in the company.

'Ah, well now, I don't really understand these things,' Carlsson said, just sufficiently aware of business dealings to know that you should never close a deal after having a few drinks.

The director was not about to let him slip that easily, however, and after half an hour Carlsson was the owner of forty shares at a hundred kronor a share in the Eagle Feldspar Co. Ltd.; he was also expressly promised the title of deputy auditor.

(Carlsson asked him to write the title down!) The matter of payment for the shares was not discussed – this was to be '*peu à peu*' and 'on account'.

After that there was coffee and brandy and punch and Bilin mineral water and it was six o'clock by the time Carlsson was ready to return to his boat.

The sailors formed up in a guard of honour as he left the ship and, since he had no idea what it meant, he shook the hands of all the men lining the gangway and invited them to pay a visit when they came ashore.

So, with his forty shares (coupons attached) in his hand, a Regalia cigar in his mouth and a basket of bottles of punch between his knees, he took the helm and had himself rowed home.

He arrived home in a state of utter bliss, treated them all to punch, even the girls in the kitchen, and showed off his share certificates, which resembled enormous bank-notes. He wanted to invite the professor over and when the others suggested it was inappropriate he pointed out that a deputy auditor was every bit as good as a German fiddler, who was not an academic and therefore not a real professor. His plans were out of this world: he was going to found a single huge herring salting plant for all the islands, bring in coopers from England and charter vessels to import salt direct from Spain. In the same breath he talked about primary industries and their representatives and expressed his fears and hopes for the future. They all sat drinking his punch, wreathed in clouds of tobacco smoke and drifting among happy mirages of Hemsö's splendid future.

Carlsson was now floating somewhere up in the clouds, living on the dizzying heights of a mountain-top. Primary industries were pushed into the background and he took to visiting Rågholmen daily. He got to know the manager and sat on his veranda drinking brandy and Bilin water while watching the workmen smashing rocks to remove the veins of quartz that were the main obstacle to shipping out the whole cliff in one or two shipments. The manager was an ex-superintendent of mines with enough experience to know how long this business was likely to last – but with enough common sense to keep on the right side of a man who was both a shareholder and deputy auditor.

The establishment of the quarry could not fail to have an impact on the physical and moral welfare of the Hemsö islanders, and the effect of the presence of thirty unmarried workmen soon became evident.

The calm of the island was disturbed. All day long thunderous detonations could be heard from the quarry; steamers hooted out in the sound; launches arrived, pulled alongside and spewed out seamen by the dozen; the workmen came over to the farm in the evening, strolled around the well and the barn keeping an eye out for the girls, organising dances, drinking with the lads and sometimes fighting. The people on the farm caroused at night and were fit for nothing during the day; they fell asleep out in the meadow and nodded and dozed in front of the stove. Every so often the manager came over to visit, which meant that the coffee pot would go on, and since it was out of the question to offer schnapps to a man of his standing they needed to have brandy in the house. But there was a market for their fish and their butter, so the money poured in and they lived high, with meat appearing on the table more often than before.

Carlsson was beginning to get fat and spent most of the day slightly inebriated, though rarely going too far. The summer passed in one long celebration, his days divided between his communal duties, quarrying and prettifying the grounds round the cottage.

With the arrival of autumn he went away for a week to carry out fire inspections and on arriving home early one morning he was met by his wife with the disturbing news that something must have happened out on Rågholmen. Not a whisper had been heard from the island for four days, not a single detonation, not a single steamer's whistle. The Hemsö people themselves had been busy with the threshing and had not found time to go out to the quarry, but there had been no sign of the manager and the workmen had stopped spending their evenings hanging about on Hemsö. Something must have happened and, intent on finding out what, Carlsson 'harnessed the horses', as he called it whenever he got the men to row him out to the quarry. He had had the boat painted white with a blue stripe and in order to give himself a more commanding appearance at the helm he had used old curtain cords to construct a pulley system that allowed him to steer while sitting upright. He had also trained Rundqvist and Norman to row in proper naval style so that their progress looked more impressive.

They made the trip quickly, spurred on by curiosity and anxiety, and when they drew level with Rågholmen they were amazed at the desolation they found there.

It was as silent as the grave, with not a soul to be seen. They went ashore and climbed up over the splinters of stone to the quarry. The manager's cottage was gone, as were all the tools and gear, and only the workmen's shed – the barracks as it had been known – remained, though it had been stripped bare and everything moveable removed, including the doors, windows, benches and bunks.

'I reckon they've gone and packed it in!' Rundqvist exclaimed.

'Looks like it!' Carlsson responded, harnessing the horses again and getting them to row him to Dalarö where he was sure there must be mail waiting for him at the post office.

There was. At the post office was a fat letter from the director, who explained that in view of the unsuitability of the raw material the company had terminated its activities on Rågholmen. Furthermore, since the four thousand kronor due to Carlsson equalled the value of the forty shares he had signed up to but omitted to pay for, there remained no further outstanding business between the company and the aforesaid Carlsson and his associates.

'Done out of four thousand!' Carlsson thought. 'And I'll just have to put up with it.'

And like a seabird, even though he was a landlubber, he shook himself dry –and felt drier still once he had read the postscript that stated that everything left behind on Rågholmen belonged to the owners of Hemsö, if they felt like taking it away.

Carlsson returned home more than a little humbled, having been fleeced of a bundle of money and stripped of his glorious title. Gusten tried to rub salt into the wound by probing into the business but Carlsson swept the whole thing aside with an airy gesture.

'Hm! Worth talking about? Nothing there to talk about!'

The following day, however, saw him and his three men hard at work with the big barge fetching planks and bricks from Rågholmen. Before anyone knew what was happening he had built a summer cabin with one room and a kitchen at a spot down by the sound that no one had considered before but from where there was a view of both the farm and the firth.

The summer with all its castles in the air was over. Winter was just round the corner and, as the air grew heavier, dreams grew darker. Reality took on a new appearance, brighter for some, more threatening for others.

CHAPTER VII

Carlsson's dreams come true; a watch is kept over the bureau, but the administrator comes and draws a line under everything.

Carlsson's marriage, though short, could not have been described as happy. The old woman was getting on, though not exactly aged, and Carlsson himself was entering those dangerous years. For most of his forty years he had been forced to toil for his daily bread and make his own way in the world, and he had failed to win the girl he wanted. But now that he had gained his ends and could look forward to a peaceful old age, the demands of the body were becoming insistent – stronger, in fact, than before, perhaps because his work over the last year had been less strenuous and perhaps, too, because he had made more provision for the flesh than the flesh could tolerate. Whenever he sat in the warmth of the kitchen his mind would begin to play with such thoughts and his eyes took to following Clara's young body as she passed in and out of the parlour. His eyes would linger a while, look down and rest, make small excursions here and there, dart away and return. Eventually the girl became fixed in his mind's eye and he saw her wherever he went. But someone else was watching too, not watching Clara but watching Carlsson's eyes following the girl, and the more she saw, the more she thought she saw, until her own eye ached and ran as if she had a sty in it.

It was a few days before Christmas Eve. Darkness had fallen but the moon had risen and shone brightly over the snow-covered spruces, the shining bay and the white ground. A bitter north wind was blowing, sweeping the dry snow before it. Clara was in the kitchen lighting the baking oven and Lotten was kneading the dough.

Carlsson was sitting by the cupboard in the corner, smoking his pipe and purring like a cat in the warmth. His eyes were roving, relishing and warmly caressing Clara's white arms where they emerged from her smock.

'Are you going to do the milking before we clean up?' Lotten asked her.

'Yes, I'll do it,' Clara answered, putting away the rake and brush and donning a sheepskin jacket.

Then she lit the byre lantern and went out – and once she had gone Carlsson stood up and followed her out.

A little while later the old woman came out of the parlour and asked where Carlsson was.

'He went out to the byre after Clara,' Lotten answered.

Without waiting to hear any more, the old woman took a lantern and went out.

There was a bitter wind blowing outside but since it was no more than a stone's throw to the byre she did not go back to put on something warm. The rocky slopes were slippery and the spindrift whirled round her like flour but she soon reached the byre and got quickly inside where it was warm. She stopped to listen and could hear whispering coming from the sheep-pen. In the weak moonlight that managed to filter through the cobwebs and hay-dust on the window-panes she saw the cows turning their heads to look at her, their great eyes shining a greenish colour in the darkness. The milking-stool was there and the pail, but that was not what she wanted to see. It was something else, something that she would have given anything not to see, something that – like witnessing an execution – attracted her at the same time as frightening the life out of her.

She moved on through the byre, climbing over heaps of straw until she came to the sheep. It was dark and quiet in there – the lantern had been extinguished but the candle itself was still smoking. The sheep were pushing and huddling and rustling their bedding of dried foliage. But they were not what she wanted to see. She moved on again and came to the hens, which had crept up on their perches and were clucking quietly as if they had just been woken up.

The door beyond was open outwards and she went out into the moonlight again. The snow revealed the tracks of two pairs of shoes, one smaller, one larger; in the shadows the tracks looked bluish and they led to the hurdle across the entrance to the paddock. The hurdle had been moved aside. She followed as if she were being dragged along, the tracks in the snow acting like a windlass chain to which she had been tied and which was now being wound in from some invisible point in the paddock.

And the chain pulled and pulled, pulling her into the same paddock, over the same stile and under the same hazel bushes where on another occasion – another dreadful occasion – she had lived through an evening hour she did not want to remember. Now the hazels were bare, bearing only their first, small, cabbage-worm catkins, and the oaks were leafless apart from a few hard brown leaves that rustled in the wind and were so sparse that the stars and the greenish-black sky were visible through them.

The chain continued, more chain, yet more chain, winding in under the spruce trees, which dropped snow on her thin grey hair when she brushed into them, snow that slithered down on her striped woollen bodice, powdering her neck and back and wetting and chilling her.

Deeper and deeper she pushed into the wood, where the capercailzie flew from its night's perch and startled her; and on beyond, out over the bog where the unstable tussocks quaked, over fences that creaked as she climbed them.

The tracks went on, two by two, one pair small, the other large, sometimes side by side, sometimes stepping in one another, sometimes around one another as if in a dance, on, on, out across the stubble field, which the wind had blown clear of snow, on over cairns and ditches, on over stacks of fence-posts and wind-fallen trees.

She did not know how long she had been walking but her head felt frozen and her thin red hands were so numb she blew on them and put them under her skirts. She would have turned back but it was too late because she would have just as far to go back as to carry on. So she went on, through a copse of aspen trees where the remaining leaves shivered and trembled as if frozen by the north wind, until she came to a stile. In the clear, sharp moonlight she could see that they had sat down there: she noticed the imprint of Clara's skirt and of the jacket with the sheepskin edging. So this was the place! Here! Her knees trembled and she froze as if her blood had become ice – and burned at the same time as if there was boiling water running through her veins. She sat down on the stile exhausted, wept, screamed, suddenly calmed down and got up and climbed over. On the other side of the stile the bay lay black and shining and across it she could see the lights in the cottage and a light up in the byre. The wind was blowing bitterly and she could feel it cutting right through her, tugging at her wispy hair and freezing her nostrils. Half running she went down onto the ice, skidded out on to its swaying surface, heard the dried reeds swish past her ears and crackle under her feet, tripped over a buoy frozen into the ice, got up again and ran as if death were at her heels and scorching her back. She reached the other shore but went right through the ice which, because of the receding water, had settled like panes of glass on the muddy bottom. With a splintering crash it broke under her weight. She felt the chill creeping up her legs but could not bring herself to scream in case anyone should come and ask her where she had been. Coughing as though her chest was about to burst she dragged herself clear of the broken ice, crawled up the slope, went straight to the bed in the parlour and told Lotten to light the fire and to make a pot of elderflower tea. And there she lay.

She asked Lotten to undress her, cover her with blankets and sheepskins and light a log fire, but she was still shaking with cold. Then she sent for Gusten, who was sitting in the kitchen.

'Are you ill, mother?' he asked in his usual unemotional way.

'I'm nearing the end,' the old woman panted. 'I shan't come through this. Shut the door and go into the bureau. The key's behind the powder horn on the shelf.'

Filled with dismay Gusten obeyed her.

'Open the lid. Pull out the third drawer on the left and take out that big letter. Good – now put it on the fire.'

Gusten obeyed and the letter flared up on the hearth, first crumpling and then crumbling to black ashes.

'Shut the door, my boy, and lock the bureau again. And keep the key. Now sit here and listen to me because I shan't be able to speak by tomorrow.'

Gusten sat down and cried a little, for now he could hear she was serious.

'As soon as my eyes are closed for ever, take the wax and your father's seal – you already have it – and go round and seal all the keyholes until the administrators come.'

'And Carlsson?' her son asked with some hesitation.

'He'll have maintenance rights – I don't think anyone can take them away from him. But not a penny more! And if you can buy him out, do so! May God be with you, Gusten. You could have come to the wedding properly but I suppose you had your reasons. Just listen to me now, you are to be sensible when I'm gone: none of these lined coffins with silver-plate mountings. Just get one of those yellow stained ones they have down on Slussplan, and not too many people, either. But I want the bells, and if the minister wants to say a few words then that's fine – you can give him your father's meerschaum pipe with the silver ferrule, and a side of mutton for his wife. And Gusten, you need to think about getting married. Find a girl you like and stick to her, but find one of your own kind, and if she's got a bit of money, so much the better. Don't marry below yourself – that sort will just eat you out of house and home: remember that birds of a feather should flock together. Now, if you'll read to me a little, I'll see if I can get some sleep.'

The door opened and Carlsson slipped in, meek but full of confidence.

'If you're ill, Anna Eva,' he said quickly, 'we should send for the doctor'.

'No need for that,' she answered and turned her face to the wall.

Carlsson suspected how the land lay and wanted to be friends again.

'Are you angry with me, Anna Eva? It really isn't worth getting upset about nothing. Do you want me to read to you from the Good Book?'

'No need for that!' was all the old woman had to say.

Carlsson, who saw that there was nothing more to be done and who did not believe in wasting effort, accepted things as they were and sat down on the settle to wait.

Since matters had already been decided and the old woman had neither the desire nor the strength to say what she was thinking, there was nothing for Carlsson to add. As for things between Gusten and himself, they could all be sorted out later. No one gave much thought to fetching a doctor because people out here expected to die unaided and, in any case, all links to the mainland were cut off.

For the next two days and nights Carlsson and Gusten kept watch over the bedroom and over each other; when one of them fell asleep on the chair or sofa the other would cat-nap with one eye open, but as soon as one moved the other would jerk awake.

By the morning of Christmas Eve Madame Carlsson was dead.

For Gusten it was as if the umbilical cord had been cut at last, as if he had been pulled from his mother's womb and become an independent being. After he had closed the old woman's eyes and put the hymn book under her chin to prevent her mouth falling open he lit a candle, took the seal and sealing wax and, in Carlsson's presence, sealed up the bureau.

Passions that had long been suppressed now came to the surface. Carlsson went and stood with his back to the bureau.

'Hey, what do you think you're doing, boy?' he said.

'I'm not a boy any longer,' Gusten answered, 'I am the farmer on Hemsö and you merely have maintenance rights!'

'Hm, two can play at that game!' Carlsson said.

Gusten took the gun down from the wall, cocked it so that the percussion cap showed, slapped the butt and roared for the first time in his life:

'Get out! Get out before I shoot you!'

'Are you threatening me?'

'Yes, and there aren't any witnesses!' Gusten answered. He had clearly been talking to people with some knowledge of law.

That was a straight answer and Carlsson knew it.

'Just you wait until the reading of the will!' Carlsson said and went out to the kitchen.

It was a gloomy Christmas Eve, what with a corpse in the house and no possibility of sending for a coffin or having the body laid out. It was snowing continuously and the ice in the bays and straits would neither bear any weight nor be open enough for sailing. The water was just a mass of slush, across which it was impossible to walk, ski or row a boat.

Carlsson and Flod (as Gusten now insisted on being called) steered clear of one another and did not exchange a word even when they shared mealtimes at the same table. The whole house was in disorder and no one took charge of the work, with the result that everyone left things to everyone else and little was done.

Christmas Day arrived, grey, misty and with more snow. Getting to church was impossible, as was getting anywhere else, so Carlsson read a sermon in the kitchen instead. Everyone felt the presence of the corpse and any Christmas spirit was out of the question. The food was prepared in a slapdash manner, nothing was ready on time and everyone was dissatisfied. The atmosphere indoors and outdoors was permeated by a dull sense of apprehension and, with the old woman's body lying in the parlour, they were all cooped up in the kitchen. They were like soldiers in a billet – when they were not eating or drinking they were sleeping, one on a sofa, another on a bed, and no one even thought of taking out the accordion or a pack of cards.

Boxing Day came and went in the same dull, tedious way but by now Flod was becoming impatient. Recognising that any further delay would lead to an unpleasant situation since the corpse was beginning to go off, he took Rundqvist with him to the work-shed, where they built a coffin and painted it yellow before using whatever they could find in the house as a shroud for the dead woman. The fifth day dawned and as the weather showed no sign of improvement – indeed, there were prospects of them having to wait another fortnight – they had to try to get the body to the church for burial at any price. They pushed the large herring-boat down into the sea and all the men collected their gear – sledges, ice-picks, axes and ropes – ready for the icy voyage. Early on the sixth day they set off on their perilous journey. Where the current had opened channels through the ice, they rowed; when they came to frozen waters, they had to haul the boat up on to sledges and drag it; worst of all was the mush-ice, in which the oars would simply splash up and down without moving the boat forward more than a few inches at a time. In some places the men preferred to walk in front and hack out a channel with their picks and axes, but woe betide anyone who cut too far beyond the channel into places where a current may have eaten its way through the thin crust.

It was already afternoon and only one more bay remained to be crossed and they had not yet taken time to eat and drink. An enormous snow-field stretched before them as far as the eye could see, broken only here and there by the small rounded mounds formed by snow-covered skerries. The eastern sky was blue-black and threatened more snow. Crows came flying past them, moving in towards land to roost for the night, and now and then the ice crashed as if a thaw was setting in. Seals could be heard barking out at sea, but although the eastern side of the bay lay open to the sea there was no open water in sight; they were sure it was there, however, since they thought they could hear the calls of long-tailed duck in that direction. Having been cut off from the mainland for a fortnight, they did not know whether the lighthouses had been extinguished, but they assumed they would have been during the days between Christmas and New Year anyway.

'We can't go on like this,' Carlsson said. He had stayed silent most of the time.

'We have to,' Flod said, putting his shoulder to the sledge, 'but we'll get ashore on Måskläppan and get some food into us.'

They began steering their course towards a very small island in the middle of the bay.

It lay farther away than they thought and it changed shape as they moved closer, until at last it was only a cable's length away.

'Hole ahead!' yelled Norman, who was acting as look-out. 'Bear off to the left!'

The sledges turned to the left, and then to the left again, until eventually they had gone all the way round the islet. Whether it was from the heat of the sun or because of warm currents rising from the bottom, the island was surrounded by water and seemed to be unreachable on all sides, at least by sledge. Dusk was falling and a good plan was vital. Flod, who had taken command of the whole manoeuvre, immediately came up with a new plan of attack: they would slide the boat off the sledges and push it out into the water, simultaneously leaping aboard and manning the oars. Decision made, they set about doing it.

'One, two, three!' Flod gave the order. The boat shot forward, lost contact with the foremost sledge and tipped sideways, so that the coffin slid into the sea.

In their complete consternation Flod and Carlsson, who were at the stern, forgot to jump into the boat and remained standing on the edge of the ice while Norman and Rundqvist managed to scramble aboard. The coffin, which had not been tightly nailed together, quickly filled with water and sank before any of them had time to think of anything but saving themselves.

'Now we must get to the manse as quickly as possible,' Flod commanded, his present mood favouring rash action rather than clear thinking.

Carlsson objected, but when Gusten asked him whether he really thought it was preferable to spend the night out on the ice he had nothing more to say, particularly once he realised that there was no hope of them reaching the small island.

Rundqvist and Norman, however, had succeeded in scrambling ashore and were yelling and shouting to their companions to follow them. Flod's only response was to wave his hand in farewell and to point south across the bay in the direction of the manse.

Carlsson and Flod marched on in silence for some time. Gusten walked in front, testing the ice with his ice-pick to see that it would bear their weight. Carlsson followed with his collar turned up, feeling distraught at his wife's sudden and pitiful end, for which he would undoubtedly be blamed.

After they had been going for half an hour Gusten stopped to take a breather. He looked all round at the islands and shore-lines to check where they were.

'Hell, we must have gone wrong somewhere!' he growled. 'That island couldn't have been Måskläppan because it's over there,' and he pointed to the east. 'And there's the pine-tree on Gillöga.'

He pointed in the direction of the mainland, towards a long low island on which a lone pine-tree had been left standing when a wooded hillock was clear-felled. The tree stood there, its two remaining branches like a semaphore signal that acted as a well-known navigation mark.

'And over there is Trälskär.'

He was talking to himself and shaking his head.

Carlsson was becoming frightened. He was not at home out here in the skerries but he had had unlimited faith in Gusten's local knowledge. Flod, however, now seemed to have taken his bearings and, changing course, he set off in a more southerly direction.

Dusk had fallen but the snow was giving some light, enough for them to know where land was. They did not speak but Carlsson followed close in the tracks of his guide.

Suddenly Gusten stopped and listened. Carlsson's inexperienced ears heard nothing but Gusten seemed to have picked up a weak roar to the east, where a bank of clouds thicker and blacker than the veil of mist shrouding the horizon had begun to pile up.

They stood still for a while until Carlsson, too, became aware of a gentle roar and a thudding sound coming ever nearer.

'What is it?' he asked, creeping closer to Gusten.

'It's the sea! In half an hour we're going to have a snowstorm brought in by the east wind and if things go really badly the ice will start breaking up. In which case, the devil only knows what'll happen to us. Come on, get a move on!'

He set off at a trot, with Carlsson after him. The snow swished round their feet and the roar seemed to be following them.

'We've had it now!' Gusten yelled, stopping and pointing to a light that was flashing behind a small island to the south-east. 'The lighthouse has been lit, which means the sea is opening up!'

Carlsson did not fully understand the danger, but he understood that their situation must be perilous if even Gusten was frightened.

Now the east wind was catching up with them and they could see a wall of snow no more than a stone's throw away advancing on them like a dark screen; then they were enveloped in snow, falling thick, dense, as black as soot. Everything around them went dark and the light of the lighthouse, which only a moment before had been a pale and blurred mock sun showing them the way, was suddenly blotted out.

Gusten carried on running hard with Carlsson following as well as he could, but he had grown fat and was soon out of breath and unable to keep up. He called to Gusten to slow down, but Gusten had no desire to sacrifice himself: he just carried on running, running for his life. Carlsson seized the tails of Gusten's coat and begged and pleaded with him not to leave him behind, promising him all the wonders of the world, appealing to him in the names of Paradise and Purgatory, but nothing helped.

'It's every man for himself now, and God help us!' Gusten answered and told Carlsson to stay a couple of paces back as otherwise the ice might break.

It already seemed to be doing so. The noise of cracking ice

behind them was growing louder, and worse, the roar of the waves was coming so close they could hear them breaking against the skerries and the edge of the ice, waking the black-backs and herring gulls to scream in anticipation of unexpected prey.

Carlsson was panting and gasping, the distance between him and Gusten was widening and finally he was left running alone in the darkness. He came to an abrupt stop and began looking for tracks but could find none. He shouted but there was no answer. There was only loneliness, darkness, cold and water, with death in their wake.

Fear spurred his feet to run on again, faster than the snowflakes though the wind was driving them in the same direction as him. He shouted again.

This time a fleeting voice reached him through the darkness: 'Run with the wind – it will take you westwards towards the shore!' Then silence.

But Carlsson had no strength left for running. His spirit failing, he began to slow down, plodding on step by step, unable to struggle any longer; and all the time he could hear the sea at his back, roaring, groaning, snarling, in tireless pursuit of its prey for the night.

*

The Reverend Nordström had gone to bed at eight o'clock that evening and lain there reading the *Diocesan News* before falling into a deep sleep. About eleven o'clock, however, he felt his wife's elbow jabbing him in the ribs and heard her calling him:

'Erik! Erik!' he heard through his sleep.

'What is it now? Why can't you calm down, woman?' he growled, only half-awake.

'Calm down? I am calm, aren't I?'

Fearing the start of a long-winded discussion the minister hastened to assure her he had no doubts about her calmness. Then he struck a match and asked what was going on.

'There's someone shouting down in the garden. Can't you hear?'

The minister listened, putting on his spectacles so he could hear better.

'Bless my soul, so there is! Who on earth can that be?'

'Well, why don't you go and see?' his wife said, jabbing her elbow into him again.

The minister put on his long-johns and fur coat, shoved his feet into his over-boots and took his gun down from the wall. He put in a percussion cap, shook down the priming powder and went out.

'Hello there! Who's there?' he shouted.

'It's me ... Flod!' answered a dull voice behind the hedge of lilac bushes.

'What the devil's going on ... coming here at this time of night? Is your mother at death's door?'

'Much worse than that!' Gusten said in a weary voice. 'We've lost her!'

'What do you mean by lost her?'

'Yes, lost her, out at sea.'

'For Heaven's sake come on in. Don't stand out there in the cold.'

When he came into the light Gusten looked as drained as a blown egg, having had nothing to eat or drink all day and been racing for his life to stay ahead of the east wind. Once the minister had been given a breathless account of the events, he went back in to his wife and returned – after a stormy few minutes – with the key to a certain cupboard in the kitchen, to which he led his shipwrecked guest. Soon Gusten was sitting at the big kitchen table while the minister set out schnapps, lard, brawn and bread for his famished visitor.

They discussed what could be done for the men who were marooned. It would be a waste of effort to call out the islanders in the dark of night, and if they lit fires along the shore it might be dangerously misleading to ships – always assuming the firelight could penetrate the fog.

They did not think the men left on the small island were in

any great danger anyway, but things looked a good deal worse for Carlsson. Gusten was virtually certain the ice in the bay must have broken up and that Carlsson was done for by now. 'It looks,' he said, 'as if he has got his just deserts.'

Reverend Nordström objected: 'Listen to me now, Gusten, I think you've all been unfair to Carlsson and I don't know what you mean by his just deserts. Look at the state the farm was in when he took charge. Hasn't he built the place up for you? Didn't he get you summer guests and build you a new cottage? As to marrying your widowed mother, well, she wanted him. And as for asking her to make a will, there was nothing wrong in him trying though it was a bit short-sighted on her part to go along with it. Carlsson was an energetic chap and he did everything you'd have liked to do but weren't up to! Now, wouldn't you like me to make an approach to the widow in Åvassa on your behalf, she's worth every penny of eight thousand? No, you shouldn't be so unbending – your way of looking at people is not the only way.'

'But whichever way you look at it he caused my mother's death and that's not something I'm going to forget easily.'

'Rubbish, you'll forget about it when you're slipping into bed alongside a wife of your own. We can hardly be sure it was Carlsson who caused her death anyway – if your mother had put some proper clothes on before she ran outside that evening she wouldn't have caught the chill that killed her. And I don't think she took it that much to heart that he was flirting with the girl, young man that he was. Anyway, this would appear to be the end of the matter and we'll see what can be done tomorrow morning. It will be Sunday and everyone will be coming to church so we won't need to call them out specially. Go to bed now and be at peace: just remember that one man's misfortune means fortune for another.'

*

The following morning when all the church-goers were standing round outside the church, the minister arrived accompanied by Flod. Instead of going in he joined the crowd of parishioners, who already seemed to have heard what had happened. After announcing that he would not be holding a service, he called on all the men to fetch their boats and to meet at the manse jetty as soon as possible so that they could go and rescue whoever there was to be rescued. Since Carlsson, as an incomer, had not been without his enemies on the council, there was some grumbling in the background, on the pretext that they did not want to forego the Word of the Lord.

'What rubbish!' the minister said. 'Knowing you as I do, I can't believe you're all that keen to listen to the watery gruel I serve up. Are you? What do you think, Åvassa – you're so well-versed in Scripture that you can tell when I'm scraping the barrel?'

This caused some quiet amusement among the crowd and stilled at least some of the objections.

'There's another Sunday next week. Come then and I'll really lay into you, I promise you. Bring your womenfolk and I guarantee to give them the kind of scolding that'll last for a couple of months. Right now, are we agreed that we're going to pull the ox out of the pit even though it's the Sabbath?'

The crowd mumbled its agreement, having been duly absolved of any breach of the Sabbath.

Then they went their separate ways, to go home and change their clothes ready to go to sea.

The snowstorm had stopped, the wind gone round to the north and the weather was cold and clear. By the time a dozen or so herring boats set out from the minister's jetty the ice in the bay had broken up and there was a blue-black swell running around the gleaming white islands. The men had come dressed in fur-coats and sealskin caps and were carrying axes and grappling irons. Sailing was out of the question so they manned the oars, with the minister and Gusten in the first boat, rowed by four hand-picked skerrymen with Bosun Rapp as look-out and bow oarsman.

The mood was serious but not unduly sad: the sea takes little account of one life more or one life less.

The seas were running fairly high and any water that came into the boat froze at once and had to be hacked off and thrown overboard. Ice-floes, some of them with reeds, leaves and sticks ripped from the shore and frozen into them, floated past and scraped against the planking before submerging and surfacing again.

The minister sat there with his field-glasses trained on Trälskär where the Hemsö men were trapped, but occasionally, and without much hope, he scanned the bay where Carlsson had almost certainly drowned. He scoured the drifting blocks of ice for any clues – a footprint, a piece of clothing or even the corpse itself – but it was all in vain.

After rowing for a couple of hours they came to the skerry where Rundqvist and Norman, who had seen the rescue flotilla approaching in the distance, had lighted fires of rejoicing on the shore. Since their lives had never been in any real danger, their mood was more one of curiosity than excitement when the boats pulled alongside.

'Nothing for us to worry about once we had dry land under our feet!' as Rundqvist put it.

The day being short they set about raising the Hemsö boat first, after which they began dragging for the coffin.

Rundqvist claimed he could point to the exact spot since he had seen the glow of sea-fire on the water. They dragged the area time after time without bringing up anything but long strands of seaweed with mussels and other creatures attached. They carried on dragging the whole morning and by noon had still not had any success. The men were beginning to look tired and despondent. Some of them had gone ashore for a dram and a sandwich and to make coffee when Gusten finally said he thought they had done all that could be done and the coffin had probably been carried out into the deep by the currents.

The men felt a general sense of relief at being spared the embarrassment of appearing unsympathetic to the troubles of others: none of them was particularly keen to see the corpse float up and the whole business, strictly speaking, was of no personal concern to them.

In order to provide a conclusion of sorts in spite of the dismal failure of their efforts, Reverend Nordström went up to Flod and asked if he would like something done to observe his mother's passing. The minister had the book with him and they could certainly come up with a hymn they all knew by heart. Gusten accepted the suggestion with gratitude and the men were told what was to be done.

The sun was coming to the end of its short journey and the skerries lay rose-red in its last light as the men gathered on the shore to take part in the unusual funeral service circumstances had forced on them. The minister, accompanied by Gusten, stepped down into a boat, went to the stern and took out his book. Holding his handkerchief between the fingers of his left hand, he bared his head and all the men on the shore followed suit and removed their caps.

'Let us take Hymn 452, "I go to meet my death". Do you know it by heart?' the minister asked.

'Yes!' the men on the shore answered.

And so the sound of their singing rose, quivering from the cold at first but then trembling with the emotions stirred by the unusual ceremony and the moving tones of the old hymn that had accompanied so many to their final rest.

The last notes rang out, echoing and fading over the water, out through the cold air, out to the skerries. Then there was a pause during which the only sounds were the soughing of the north wind through the needles of the dwarf pines, the splashing of the waves on the rocks, the cries of the gulls and the bumping of the boats against the bottom. The minister turned his furrowed old face out towards the bay and the sun shone on his bald head, around which the wisps of grey hair fluttered like lichen hanging on an ancient spruce-tree.

'"Earth to earth, ashes to ashes, dust to dust; in the sure and certain hope of the Resurrection to eternal life, through Jesus Christ our Lord." Let us pray,' the minister began in his deep voice, which had to fight against the wind and the waves to be heard.

And so the burial service continued, ending with the Lord's

Prayer, and after the blessing the minister stretched his hand out over the waters in one last farewell.

The men put on their caps. Gusten pressed the minister's hand and thanked him, but he still seemed to have something on his mind.

'Minister, I wonder ... do you think we should perhaps have a few words for Carlsson, too?'

'I was speaking for both of them, dear boy, but it was generous of you to think of him,' the old man replied, seeming more moved by this than he might have wished.

The sun went down and it was time for them to part and try to get home as quickly as they could.

They wanted, however, to give Flod one last mark of respect so, once they had all exchanged farewells and were back in their boats, they accompanied him part of the way, their boats arrayed in line as when setting out the herring nets. Then they raised their oars in salutation and shouted goodbye.

It was a token of sorrow but also of the acceptance of the young man into the self-reliant ranks of the men of the islands.

And so, sitting at the helm of his own boat, the new master of Hemsö was rowed home by his men, to begin piloting his own vessel across the windy bays and through the green straits of this uncertain life.

AFTERWORD

We would be hard put to find an opening with more pace and humour than *The People of Hemsö*, one of Strindberg's many great set-pieces: 'He came like a snowstorm one April evening and had an earthenware jug hanging on a strap round his neck. Clara and Lotten had gone in the herring boat to pick him up but it was ages before they got back to the boat'. In a letter to his publisher Albert Bonnier Strindberg called the novel 'an intermezzo scherzando between the battles', the battles being – in a literary sense, anyway – his play *The Father* (1887) and the novel *A Madman's Defence* (1887-88), but *The People of Hemsö* shows little trace of the mental and marital turmoil that was going on round it.

August Strindberg was born in Stockholm in 1849 into a well-off bourgeois family though he frequently preferred, as in the title of his autobiographical novel *Tjänstekvinnans son* (Son of a Serving Woman, 1886), to stress the less elevated social origins of his mother. After trying his hand first as a medical student and then as an apprentice actor at the Royal Dramatic Theatre he became a student of aesthetics at the University of Uppsala in 1867. His first play to be produced, *Fritänkaren* (The Freethinker), was staged in 1870 while he was still a student but he left the university in 1872 without completing his studies, which is perhaps less than surprising given that he had written no fewer than six plays in that time, including his first major drama *Mäster Olof* (Master Olof, 1872). An historical drama set at the time of the Swedish Reformation in the sixteenth century, *Mäster Olof* was rejected by the Royal Theatre and, in spite of several revisions and rewrites, not produced until 1881. Returning to Stockholm, Strindberg earned his living as a free-lance writer, journalist and later librarian, living in the poorer quarters of the city in a bohemian milieu of artists and writers. These are the years that provided the material for *Röda rummet* (The Red Room, 1879), his first novel and his literary breakthrough. In 1877 he had married the Finland-Swedish aristocrat Siri von Essen after a tangled courtship that involved Siri divorcing her first husband. The couple and their three children then spent the greater part of the 1880s outside Sweden in France, Switzerland, Germany and latterly Denmark, and it was during this period of exile that the great trio of naturalistic dramas – *Fadren* (The Father, 1887), *Fröken Julie* (Miss Julie, 1888) and *Fordringsägare* (Creditors, 1888) – were written. The struggle for power between the sexes, at least partly a reflection of his own marital turmoil, lies at the heart of these plays – and they gained him his lasting reputation as a misogynist. But during the same period he wrote, often reluctantly and in haste since they took him away from the serious work of drama, the novels and short stories necessary to financial survival – *Hemsöborna* (The People of Hemsö, 1887), *Skärkarlsliv* (Life in the Skerries, 1888) and *I havsbandet* (By the Open Sea, 1890). And in 1887-88 he also wrote (in French) the savage autobiographical novel *En dåres försvarstal* (A Madman's Defence) with its paranoid attacks on his wife Siri. On his return to Sweden in 1889 he settled in the Stockholm Archipelago, but following the final bitter break-up of his first marriage he moved abroad again in 1892, first to Berlin, thereafter to Austria during his short-lived second marriage to the Austrian journalist Frida Uhl, and finally to Paris. These years of renewed exile are marked by financial penury, spiritual crisis and the psychological breakdown that led to his desertion of literature for the pseudo-sciences of alchemy and occultism. He describes this time in the autobiographical novel *Inferno* (1897), which marks his return to literature and introduces the period of the great and formally pioneering dramas of spiritual search, conversion and, intermittently, reconciliation: *Till Damaskus I-II* (To Damascus, 1898), *Advent* (1898) and *Ett drömspel* (A Dream Play, 1901). He returned to Stockholm in

154

1899, married the young actress Harriet Bosse a few years later but separated in 1904. He remained in Stockholm for the rest of his life, still writing prolifically in both prose and dramatic forms and involved in running and writing for his own small theatre. During these years he also returned to radical journalism. He died in 1912 and his funeral drew a crowd of sixty thousand.

Recognised internationally as one of the world's great dramatists, Strindberg is less well known outside Sweden for the range of his other creative work—novels, short stories, essays, journalism, poetry, and his paintings, which in recent decades have received the critical attention they merit. His ability to spark controversy on the issues of the day was enormous, as was his productivity: the National Edition of his collected works, now approaching completion, will run to seventy-two volumes; the publication of his collected letters fills twenty-two volumes.

*

In *The People of Hemsö* we find Strindberg, as so often, making close use of autobiographical or self-observed material. From 1871 to 1883, at first as a bachelor and then with his wife Siri and their young family, Strindberg spent most of his summers in rented farmhouses on the small island of Kymmendö in the Stockholm Archipelago. These summers were without doubt his happiest times and the novels and stories he set among the islands reveal his familiarity with and great affection for the region. It is perhaps not surprising, then, that in Lindau on Lake Constance, after four years of exile, with his marriage on the rocks and his finances in disarray, his memory returned to Kymmendö and happier days. In the story Kymmendö became Hemsö and was moved a little farther from the mainland but, in spite of name changes, the identities of the characters he depicted in his novel were utterly transparent and the islanders he described were so incensed that he was never again welcome to visit the island. (In two cases he effectively left the names the same: Clara remained Clara and Lotta merely became Lotten.)

In a recent essay on Strindberg and the archipelago Ludvig Rasmusson writes: 'For me, *The People of Hemsö* is the Great Swedish Novel, just as *Madame Bovary* is the Great French Novel and *The Adventures of Huckleberry Finn* the Great American Novel'. We don't have to agree with Rasmusson on the issue of 'greatness' in order to know exactly what he means: just as the Mississippi becomes the quintessence of America, Hemsö and the archipelago become the quintessence of Sweden. The visual quality of the narration is such that we move through a rolling series of peopled panoramas in which place and time and character are somehow simultaneously specific and archetypical, and we leave the novel with memories of grand landscapes and spirited scenes, an epic tapestry of that imagined, and perhaps imaginary, space that is Sweden: the boat journey through the islands with which the novel opens, the haymaking, the wedding, the quarrying company's inaugural breakfast, Madame Flod's pursuit of Carlsson and Lotten through the chill winter night, the pastor and Gusten at the fisherman's bothy in the outer skerries, and – perhaps most unforgettable of all – the journey across the breaking sea-ice with Madame Flod's coffin and Carlsson's lonely final moments. Strindberg's own view of the novel alternated between the slightly grandiose ('my novel is intended as a work of art' – though, to be fair, he was trying to sell it at that point) and scoffing at it as a piece of hack work ('I'm currently writing an idyll even more idiotic than *The People of Hemsö*'). But the novel is far from being an idyll, just as it is far from being a condescending comedy of peasant manners, which is not to say that it does not have flashes of both. It is, perhaps, best described as a naturalistic tragicomedy. Naturalistic because of its wonderful detail of fishing and farming, of birds and of flowers – details which in Strindberg's hands become active participants in the narrative rather than dry lists to suggest verisimilitude. Naturalistic, too, in the conflict between Carlsson and Gusten, the farmer and the hunter, and in the contrast between town and country, culture and nature. Tragic because Madame Flod/Carlsson and Carlsson himself do not only lose their lives, their decease is preceded by the loss of their dreams and aspirations. But all this is ruled by humour – burlesque, caricature, situational, wit, satire – and, what is rare in Strindberg's writing, it is the humour of compassion: this narrative is free of illusions, but it is equally untouched by cynicism. Then, of course, there is Strindberg's language. The breadth of his vocabulary is astonishing, as is his precision in using it, but much more breathtaking than that is his mastery of cadence and tempo: read again any of the great set-piece scenes and observe how the pace swells and ebbs, ebbs and swells as the narrative proceeds.

*

Given its lasting public popularity, *The People of Hemsö* has appeared in several different guises. Strindberg himself dramatised it in the form of a 'folk comedy' in 1889 – a process that he described in a letter to Ola Hansson as making him 'feel like a whore' and that Martin Lamm described as a 'vandalisation of the text'. The novel has been filmed three times: in 1919 (silent), directed by Carl Barcklind; in 1944, directed by Sigurd Wallén; and in 1955, directed by Arne Mattsson. In 1966 Swedish television adapted the novel as a seven-part serialisation and, more recently, the composer Georg Riedel has turned the novel into an opera premiered at Folkoperan in Stockholm in 1994.

Since its publication in 1887 the novel has been translated into twenty-five languages. The first translations to appear were Dutch (1890), Czech (1892), German (1894 –there have been six different translations into German in all), Polish (1895) and French (1897). Following that initial flurry, no further translations appeared until the 1920s. The novel did not appear in English until 1959.

There have been two earlier translations into English: *The People of Hemsö,* translated by Elspeth Harley Schubert, (London: Jonathan Cape, 1959), and *The Natives of Hemsö,* translated by Arvid Paulson, (New York: Paul S. Eriksson, 1965). The present translation has been made from August Strindberg, *Hemsöborna* (with commentary by Gunnar Lokrantz) (Stockholm: Svenska Bokförlaget/Bonniers, 1964), which follows the text published in August Strindberg, *Samlade skrifter 21: Hemsöborna och Skärkarlsliv,* edited by John Landquist (Stockholm: Bonniers, 1918).

I should like to thank Helena Forsås-Scott for her warm encouragement, detailed reading and many helpful suggestions.

Peter Graves
Edinburgh, January 2012

AUGUST STRINDBERG

Strindberg's One-Act Plays: A Selection

Simoom, Facing Death, The Outlaw, The Bond

(translated by Agnes Broomé, Anna Holmwood,
John K Mitchinson, Mathelinda Nabugodi,
Anna Tebelius and Nichola Smalley)

To most English-language readers and theatre goers, Strindberg is mainly known for naturalistic plays such as *Miss Julie* and *The Father*, but the dramatic production of Sweden's national playwright is infinitely richer and more extensive than these would suggest. This volume presents four of Strindberg's lesser known one act plays, *The Bond*, *Facing Death*, *The Outlaw* and *Simoom*, written between 1871 and 1892, which showcase Strindberg's remarkable range. *The Bond* and *Facing Death*, which fall at the end of the time span, are familiarly naturalistic plays set in contemporary European settings which demonstrate Strindberg's provocative engagement with contentious issues of his day. The early experiment *The Outlaw*, however, takes place in the frigid landscapes of the Viking north, drawing heavily on the style of Icelandic sagas. In Simoom, written in 1889, a practically gothic narrative transports us to the scorching deserts of French colonised Algeria, allowing us to observe the beginnings of Strindberg's experimental, mystical phase which culminated in A Dream Play. Different as the four plays are, however, when read together they form a thematic unity, revealing the beating heart of Strindberg's creativity, the issue at the core of his writing: love as a war eternally waged man and woman, husband and wife, children and parents and individuals and society.

ISBN 9781870041935
UK £9.95
(Paperback, 128 pages)

JONAS LIE

The Family at Gilje

(translated by Marie Wells)

Captain Jæger is the well-meaning but temperamental head of a rural family living in straitened circumstances in 1840s Norway. The novel focuses on the fates of the women of the family: the heroic Ma, who struggles unremittingly to keep up appearances and make ends meet, and their eldest daughter Thinka, forced to renounce the love of her life and marry an older and wealthier suitor. Then there is the younger daughter, the talented and beautiful Inger-Johanna, destined to make a splendid match – but will the captain with the brilliant diplomatic career ahead of him make her happy? With great empathy and affection for each member of the family Lie evokes the tragedy of hopes dashed by the harsh social and economic realities of the day, and the influence of one person who dares to think differently. Both in the landscape and in the characters the wildness of nature is played out against the constraints of culture.

ISBN 9781870041942
UK £14.95
(Paperback, 210 pages)

SELMA LAGERLÖF

Nils Holgersson's Wonderful Journey

(translated by Peter Graves)
Volume 1: ISBN 9781870041966
Volume 2: ISBN 9781870041973
UK £12.95 per volume
(Paperback)
Coming out in December 2012

Lord Arne's Silver

(translated by Sarah Death)
ISBN 9781870041904
UK £9.95
(Paperback, 102 pages)

The Phantom Carriage

(translated by Peter Graves)
ISBN 9781870041911
UK £11.95
(Paperback, 126 pages)

The Löwensköld Ring

(translated by Linda Schenk)
ISBN 9781870041928
UK £9.95
(Paperback, 120 pages)

Selma Lagerlöf (1858-1940) quickly established herself as a major author of novels and short stories, and her work has been translated into close to 50 languages. Most of the translations into English were made soon after the publication of the original Swedish texts and have long been out of date. 'Lagerlöf in English' provides English-language readers with high-quality new translations of a selection of the Nobel Laureate's most important texts.

Printed in July 2019
by Rotomail Italia S.p.A., Vignate (MI) - Italy